THE CAT WHO
BROUGHT DOWN THE HOUSE

Also available from Isis Large Print:

THE CAT WHO BROUGHT DOWN THE HOUSE

Lilian Jackson Braun

ISIS
LARGE PRINT
Oxford

First published in Great Britain 2003
by Headline Book Publishing Ltd

Published in Large Print 2003 by ISIS Publishing Ltd,
7 Centremead, Osney Mead, Oxford OX2 0ES
by arrangement with
Headline Book Publishing Ltd, a division of Hodder Headline

British Library Cataloguing in Publication Data
Braun, Lilian Jackson
The cat who brought down the house.
– Large print ed.
1. Qwilleran, Jim (Fictitious character) – Fiction
2. Detective and mystery stories
3. Large type books
I. Title
813.5'4 [F]

ISBN 0–7531–6843–X (hb)
ISBN 0–7531–6844–8 (pb)

Printed and bound by Antony Rowe, Chippenham

Dedicated to Earl Bettinger,
The Husband Who . . .

CHAPTER
ONE

Who was Thelma Thackeray?

It was April first, and it sounded like an April Fool's joke.

Had anyone by that name ever lived in Moose County, 400 miles north of everywhere?

Yet, there it was, in black and white — in the newsbite column of the *Moose County Something*:

RETURN OF THE NATIVE

Thelma Thackeray, 82, a native of Moose County, has retired after a 55-year career in Hollywood, CA, and is returning to her native soil. "I'm coming home to die," she said cheerfully, "but not right away. First I want to have some fun."

It was followed by less startling items: The sheriff had purchased a stop-stick to aid deputies in high-speed car chases . . . The Downtown Beautiful committee had decided on hot-pink petunias for the flower boxes on Main Street . . . The sow that escaped from a truck on Sandpit Road had been discovered in the basement of the Black Creek Elementary School.

Immediately the lead item was being discussed all over town, via the grapevine. In coffeehouses, on street corners, and over backyard fences the news was spread: "A Hollywood star is coming to live in Pickax!"

Jim Qwilleran, columnist for the newspaper, was working at home when his phone started ringing. "Who was Thelma Thackeray? . . . Was she really a movie star? . . . Did the press know more than they were telling?"

"It sounds like a hoax," he told them. He remembered the April Fool's prank that his fellow staffers had played on the *Lockmaster Ledger* a year ago. They phoned a tip that a Triple Crown winner was being retired to a stud farm in Lockmaster under terms of absolute secrecy. Reporters at the *Ledger* had spent a week trying to confirm it.

Nevertheless, Qwilleran's curiosity was aroused. He phoned Junior Goodwinter, the young managing editor, and said sternly, "What was the source of the Thelma Thackeray newsbite?"

"She phoned our night desk herself — from California. Why do you ask? Do you have a problem with that?"

"I certainly do! The name sounds phony! And her remark about dying and having fun is too glib for a person of her apparent age."

"So what are you telling me, Qwill?"

"I'm telling you it's a practical joke played by those guys in Lockmaster in retaliation for the horse hoax. Have you been getting any reader reaction?"

"Sure have! Our phones have been ringing off the hook! And — hey, Qwill! Maybe there really is a Thelma Thackeray!"

"Want to bet?" Qwilleran grumbled as he hung up.

Qwilleran had a sudden urge for a piece of Lois Inchpot's apple pie, and he walked to the shabby downtown eatery where one could always find comfort food at comfortable prices — and the latest gossip. Lois herself was a buxom, bossy, hardworking woman who had the undying loyalty of her customers. They took up a collection when she needed a new coffeemaker and volunteered their services when the lunchroom walls needed painting.

When Qwilleran arrived, the place was empty, chairs were upended on tables, and Lois was sweeping up before dinner. "Too early for dinner! Too late for coffee!" she bellowed.

"Where's your busboy, Lois?"

Her son, Lenny, usually helped her prepare for dinner.

"Job hunting! He finished two years at MCCC, and he'd really like to go to one of them universities Down Below, but they're too expensive. So he's job hunting."

Qwilleran said, "Tell Lenny to apply to the K Fund for a scholarship. I'll vouch for him." The young man had faced personal tragedy, a frame-up, and betrayal of trust — with pluck and perseverance.

With a sudden change of heart she said, "What kind of pie do you want?"

"Apple," he said, "and give me that broom and I'll finish sweeping while you brew the coffee."

The middle-aged man pushing the broom and righting the chairs would have been recognized anywhere in three counties as James Mackintosh Qwilleran. He had a pepper-and-salt moustache of magnificent proportions, and his photo appeared at the head of the "Qwill Pen" column every Tuesday and Friday. He had been a highly regarded journalist in major cities around the country; then he inherited the vast Klingenschoen fortune based in Moose County and he relocated in the north country. Furthermore, for reasons of his own, he had turned the inheritance over to a philanthropic institution. The Klingenschoen Foundation, popularly called the K Fund, was masterminded by experts in Chicago, where Qwilleran was recognized as the richest man in the northeast central United States. Around Pickax he was Mr Q.

Eventually Lois returned from the kitchen, carrying two orders of apple pie and a coffee server; forks, napkins, and mugs were in her apron pockets. They sat in a booth near the kitchen pass-through, so she could shout reminders to the woman who cooked dinner. Lois herself would wait on tables, take the money, and serve as moderator of the free-for-all talk show carried on among the tables.

"Well, Mr Q," she began, "you missed a good chinfest this afternoon. Everybody's excited about the movie star comin' to town. Do you think she'll come in here to eat?"

Still suspecting a Lockmaster trick, he replied evasively, "Just because she's lived in Hollywood for fifty years, it doesn't make her a movie star. She could be a bookkeeper or policewoman or bank president."

Whatever she is, he thought, she must be loaded — to buy a house on Pleasant Street.

Lois shouted at the pass-through, "Effie! Don't forget to thaw the cranberry sauce! . . . Funny thing, though, Mr Q — nobody remembers a Thackeray family in these parts."

Facetiously he said, "It would be interesting to know if she's related to William Makepeace Thackeray."

"Don't know anybody of that name. Who is he?"

"A writer, but he hasn't done anything recently."

She yelled, "And, Effie! Throw some garlic powder in the mashed potatoes!"

Qwilleran said, "Sounds delicious. I'd like to take a turkey dinner home in a box."

Lois yelled, "Effie! Fix a box for Mr Q — and put in some dark meat for his kitties."

"By the way," he said, "what's all the action in the next block? All those trucks coming and going."

"They're movin' out!" she said. "Good riddance! It don't make sense to have a place like that downtown."

He waited for his "box" and walked to the corner of Church and Pine streets, where large cartons were being loaded into trucks and carted away. According to the logos on the cartons they were refrigerators, washers and dryers, kitchen ranges, and television sets.

He said to the man directing the loading, "Either you're moving out, or you've sold a lot of appliances this week."

"We got a new building on Sandpit Road — steel barn with real loading dock. Plenty of room for trucks."

The edifice they were vacating was a huge stone hulk, wedged between storefronts of more recent vintage. That meant it was more than a century old, dating back to the days when the county's quarries were going full blast and Pickax was being built as the City of Stone. It was the first time he had scrutinized it. There were no windows in the side walls, and the front entrance had been boarded up. Qwilleran crossed the street and appreciated the design for the first time: Four columns were part of the architecture, topped by a pediment and the simple words inscribed in the stone: OPERA HOUSE.

Then he realized that the smaller buildings on either side had been vacated also. Something was happening in downtown Pickax!

Qwilleran went home to his converted apple barn, which was as old as the opera house. It occupied a wooded area on the outskirts of town — octagonal, forty feet high, with fieldstone foundation and weathered wood shingles for siding. As he drove into the barnyard two alert cats were watching excitedly in the kitchen window. They were sleek Siamese with pale fawn bodies and seal-brown masks and ears, long slender legs, and whiplike tails. And they had startlingly blue eyes.

Yum Yum was a flirtatious little female who purred, rubbed ankles, and gazed at Qwilleran beseechingly with violet-tinged eyes. She knew how to get what she wanted; she was all cat . . . Koko was a cat-and-a-half. Besides being long, lithe, and muscular, he had the bluest of blue eyes, brimming with intelligence and something beyond that — an uncanny intuition. There were times when the cat knew the answers before Qwilleran had even thought of the questions. Kao K'o Kung was his real name.

When Qwilleran walked into the barn, Yum Yum was excited about the turkey, but Koko was excited about the answering machine; there was a message waiting.

A woman's voice said, "Qwill, I'm leaving the library early and going to the dinner meeting of the bird club. It's all about chickadees tonight. I'll call you when I get home and we can talk about Thelma Thackeray. *A bientôt.*"

She left no name, and none was needed. Polly Duncan was the chief woman in his life. She was his own age and shared his interest in literature, being director of the Pickax public library. It was her musical voice that had first attracted him. Even now, when she talked, he felt a frisson of pleasure that almost overshadowed what she was saying.

Qwilleran thanked Koko for drawing his attention to the message and asked Yum Yum if she had found any treasures in the wastebasket. Talking to cats, he believed, raised their consciousness.

The dark meat of turkey was minced and arranged on two plates under the kitchen table, where they gobbled it up with rapture. Afterward it took them a long time to wash up. The tastier the treat, the longer the ablutions, Qwilleran had observed.

Then he announced loudly, "Gazebo Express now leaving for all points east!" Yum Yum and Koko jumped into a canvas tote bag that had been purchased from the Pickax public library. It was the right size for ten books or two cats who are good friends.

The octagonal gazebo stood in the bird garden, screened on all eight sides. In the evening there were birds and small four-legged creatures to amuse the Siamese, and when darkness fell there were night noises and night smells. Qwilleran stayed with them for a while, then went indoors to do some more work on the "Qwill Pen" column.

From time to time he received phone calls from friends who wanted to talk about the Hollywood celebrity: from Wetherby Goode, the WPKX meteorologist; from Celia Robinson O'Dell, his favorite caterer; from Susan Exbridge, antique dealer; the Lanspeaks, owners of the department store.

At one point he was interrupted by a phone call from Lisa Compton, wife of the school superintendent.

"Lyle and I were wondering if you know what's going into the old opera house?"

"No, I know only what's coming out. Maybe they're going to bring Mark Twain back. He hasn't been here since 1895."

"I know," Lisa said. "And my grandmother was still raving about him sixty years later. She loved his moustache — just like yours, Qwill. His wit and humor brought down the house! Her favorite was the one about cross-breeding man with the cat: *It would improve the man but be deleterious to the cat.*"

8

"She told me that carriages used to draw up to the entrance of the hall, and women in furs and jewels would step out, assisted by men in opera cloaks and tall hats. Can you imagine that — in Pickax, Qwill?"

"That was over a hundred years ago," Qwilleran said. "Things change."

"So true! Before World War One the economy had collapsed. Pickax was almost a ghost town, and the opera hall was boarded up. In the Twenties it was a movie theatre for a few years. During World War Two the government took it over — all very hush-hush and heavily guarded. They removed the rows of seats and leveled the raked floor, my family told me."

Qwilleran said, "The old building has had a checkered career."

"Yes, since then it's been a roller rink, a dance hall, a health club, and finally a storage warehouse. Who knows what's next?"

"If you get any clues, let me know," he said.

"I'll do that . . . How are the kitties, Qwill?"

"Fine. How's Lyle?"

"Grouchy. He's crossing swords with the school board again."

Qwilleran was treating himself to a dish of ice cream when Polly phoned. "How was your meeting?" he asked. "What did you have for dinner?"

"Robin-O'Dell catered some meat pies. Food always suffers in the transportation, you know, but they were acceptable."

"Did you learn anything about chickadees that you didn't already know?"

She wailed in exasperation. "There was more discussion about that Thackeray woman than about birds! . . . There was one thing that I found rather amusing, though. The realty agent who sold her the house was there; he and his wife are avid birders. At first he was reluctant to talk — professional confidentiality, you know — but after a few glasses of wine he relaxed. He said she bought it sight unseen, after they sent photos and specifications . . . They lined up Mavis Adams to check legal details and Fran Brodie to handle the redecorating. In fact, Fran flew to California for a conference."

Qwilleran asked, "Did he say why she needs such a large house?"

"He claimed not to know. But it would be interesting to talk to Fran, wouldn't it?"

Feigning a lack of interest, he mumbled something and reminded Polly that they were dining with the Rikers the next night. "I've made a reservation at the Mackintosh Inn. We'll meet here at the barn at six o'clock."

"I'm looking forward to it," she said. "*A bientôt.*"
"*A bientôt.*"

Before bringing in the Siamese from the gazebo, Qwilleran flicked the single switch that lighted the entire interior of the barn with uplights and down-lights. A ramp spiraled dramatically around the inside walls, connecting the three balconies. In the

10

center of the main floor stood a giant white fireplace cube with white stacks rising to the cupola.

The Siamese were waiting, torn between the enchantment of the night and the prospect of a bedtime snack. As soon as they were indoors, they jumped out of the tote bag and raced up the ramp — Koko chasing Yum Yum all the way to the top. Then she turned and chased him down again. Qwilleran clocked them: thirty-seven seconds for the entire course.

Then the three of them piled into the big reading chair and listened to a recording of *Carmen*. It was the cats' favorite. Qwilleran liked anything by Bizet. Wouldn't it be sensational, he thought, if the old opera house started bringing in opera companies! But not impossible. Anything could happen in Pickax, 400 miles north of everywhere.

CHAPTER
TWO

Just before waking on Wednesday, Qwilleran dreamed about the old opera house. The elite of Pickax were arriving in horse-drawn carriages. Every seat in the house was taken with opera-lovers excited about hearing *Tristan and Isolde*. Then he opened his eyes! The Siamese were performing a Wagnerian duet outside his door.

Qwilleran leaped out of bed. "You demons!" he scolded. They ran down the ramp, and he took the short cut to the kitchen via a circular staircase.

He prepared the cats' breakfast absently, having two questions on his mind — both of more interest than chopped chicken livers. Who was Thelma Thackeray? he asked himself. And what was about to happen to the opera house? After a career as a warehouse for household appliances, the old building had nowhere to go but up. Suppose the K Fund were to restore it to its former glamour! Would anyone attend concerts and lectures in this age of TV and videos?

He prepared super-strength coffee in his automated brewer and thawed a breakfast roll. Then he made phone calls.

First he called Amanda's Studio of Interior Design, hoping Fran Brodie would be in-house, but she was still in California, working with the client, and Amanda was at City Hall, doing the duties of a mayor. Qwilleran left his name, and the new assistant said, "Oh! You're Mr Q! I live in Lockmaster, but I read your column in the *Something* and it's neat — really neat!"

Next he phoned the official county historian to inquire about the Thackeray family. Homer Tibbitt was ninety-eight, and he lived with his wife, Rhoda, at Ittibittiwassee Estates, a retirement residence out in the country. They were virtually newlyweds. Neither had been married before, and theirs was considered the romance of the century.

Rhoda answered the phone in her sweet trembling voice and turned it over to Homer, whose vocal delivery was reedy and high-pitched, but vigorous. "The only thing I know about the Thackeray family is that Milo was a bootlegger in the Thirties. Thornton Haggis would have all that information. He read a paper at a meeting of the historical society — all about our fair county during Prohibition."

So Qwilleran phoned the Thornton Haggis residence. Thorn, as he liked to be called, was a fourth-generation stonecutter, now retired from the family's monument works. He had a degree in art history from a university Down Below and now gave liberally of his time to the local art community. His wife told Qwilleran to call the Art Center; Thorn was helping to hang a new exhibition.

Sure enough, the volunteer was up on a ladder when Qwilleran phoned. "I can tell you a thing or two about Moose County's boozy history. Where are you, Qwill? At the barn? The job here will be finished in a half hour, and I'll drive up there. Brew some of that lethal coffee you like!"

It was generally assumed that Thornton would take over the unpaid job of county historian when, if ever, Homer retired. The records of the monument works went back to 1850, when tombstones were chiseled with name, the vital statistics, cause of death, and names of survivors and family pets. Also, examples of with and humor were chipped into the stone at modest price-per-letter.

Qwilleran's visitor had a rampant shock of snow-white hair visible a block away. The Siamese always became unusually frisky when he appeared. "Is that a compliment?" he asked. "Or do they suspect me of something?"

Qwilleran suggested, "They associate your last name with something good to eat. Cats have a clever way of putting two and two together."

"I drove around by the library and picked up the paper I wrote for the local history collection. It's the one I read at the meeting of the Old Times Club. It made some of them cry."

"Good! Let's go out to the gazebo with some refreshments, and you can read it to me. I'll take a box of tissues."

It was a pleasantly warm day — and an hour when the wild creatures were not too noisy. What looked like red wine on the refreshment tray was actually Squunk water from a local mineral spring, with a slug of cranberry juice. Thorn smacked his lips. "You could bottle this stuff and sell it!"

Qwilleran turned on his tape recorder, and the following was later transcribed for *Short & Tall Tales*, a collection of local legends.

MILO THE POTATO FARMER

Milo Thackeray and my grandfather were good friends. They played checkers and went hunting together — varmints and deer. Hunting was not a sport in those days. For many struggling families it was a way to put food on the table. Hard times had come to Moose County in the early twentieth century. Yet this had been the richest county in the state when natural resources were being exploited.

Then the ten mines closed, leaving entire villages without hope of work; the forests were lumbered out; there was no market for quarry stone; the ship-building industry went elsewhere when steamboats replaced tall-masted schooners. Thousands of persons fled Down Below, hoping to find work in factories, and those who remained had little money to spend on potatoes and tombstones. Milo was a potato farmer, and Gramps was a stonecutter.

It had been a year of tragedy for the potato farmer. His eldest son was one of the first casualties of World War One; two younger children died in the influenza epidemic; and now his wife died while giving birth to twins, Thelma and Thurston. They were his salvation! Gramps was there when Milo swore an oath to give them a better life than he had known. A sister-in-law came in to care for them, and eventually Milo married her. Eventually, too, his life took a strange turn.

In 1919 the Volstead Act went into effect, and thirsty citizens provided a large market for illegal beverages. Somehow, Milo learned he could make hard liquor from potatoes. Gramps helped him build a distillery, and it worked! Customers came to the farm in Model T cars and horse-drawn wagons. Unfortunately for the jubilant farmer, revenue agents also came. They smashed the still and poured the liquor on the ground. (Even to this day the belief persists that the act accounts for the superior flavor of Moose County potatoes.)

Milo was undaunted! His twins were growing fast, and he had sworn an oath.

Across the lake, a hundred miles away, was Canada, famous for good whiskey. On the shore of Moose County there were scores of commercial fishermen who were getting only a penny a pound for their catch. Milo organized a fleet of rumrunners to bring the whiskey over under cover of darkness. Soon a steady stream of Model T trucks was coming north to haul it away, camouflaged in many ingenious ways.

The poor potato farmer became the rich bootlegger.

Transactions were made in cash, and Gramps held the lantern while Milo buried the money in the backyard.

Every weekend Milo took his family and their young friends to Lockmaster for a picnic and moving picture show. The back of the truck was filled with kids sitting on disguised cases of contraband. Milo never attended the show, and the seats were never there for the return trip.

There was no such entertainment in Moose County. The twins begged their father to open a picture show in Pickax.

Prohibition ended in 1933, but the potato farmer was in a position to indulge his twins. He bought the old opera house, long boarded up, and made it the Pickax Movie Palace. He financed their chosen careers.

Besides their sex, the twins were very different. Thurston was slight of build and more sensitive; he loved dogs and horses and wanted to be a veterinarian. Milo sent him to Cornell, where he earned his D.V.M. degree.

Thelma was taller, huskier, and bolder; she wanted to be "in pictures." Milo sent her to Hollywood with her stepmother as chaperone. He never saw either of the women again.

Thelma obtained bit parts in two B films and decided she would prefer the food business, playing the leading role as hostess in her own restaurant. Milo first financed a snack shop (the Thackeray Snackery) and then a fine restaurant called simply Thelma's. She did very well. When Milo died he left his fortune to Thurston, to establish the Thackeray Animal Clinic in Lockmaster, and to Thelma, to realize her dream of a private dinner club for connoisseurs of old movies.

Milo was buried in the Hilltop Cemetery, with Gramps as the sole mourner. And Gramps chiseled the headstone the way his friend wanted it: MILO THE POTATO FARMER.

"Good story!" Qwilleran said as he turned off the tape recorder. "Is Thelma's twin still living?"

"No, Dr Thurston was killed in an accident a year or so ago. There was a rumor that it was murder, but no charges were brought. The gossips said that a group of horse breeders had been trying to buy the Thackeray Clinic but Thurston wouldn't sell. Right after his death they bought it from the estate and changed the name. I don't read the *Lockmaster Ledger*, so I don't know any details. But the idea of murder didn't make sense to me."

"Well, anyway, the twin sister is returning to her hometown for some 'fun,' according to an item in the *Something*."

"My wife told me about it. Am I supposed to get excited about it? Sounds to me as if she's been out in the sun too long!"

Qwilleran, although feigning a lack of interest, was beginning to have a nagging curiosity about Thelma

18

Thackeray, and he looked forward to Fran Brodie's return from California.

The Siamese knew something was about to happen — something important, not alarming. Their dinner was served early; the nut bowls on the coffee table were filled; glasses and bottles appeared on the serving bar. The cats watched the preparations, forgoing their usual postprandial meditation in a sunny spot.

Qwilleran was proud of his bartending skills, and he always served his guests with a fillip of formality. Now he had acquired a round silver tray with the merest suggestion of a fluted rim — just enough to keep it from looking like a hubcap. (He disliked anything ornate.) There were modern trays in aluminum, chrome, and stainless steel, and he had served drinks on them all, but silver had *soul*. Even the Siamese felt it. They jumped on the bar and looked at their reflections in its highly polished surface. It had been a gift from two of his favorite young people!

At six o'clock Polly Duncan was the first to drive into the barnyard, having come directly from the library. "You have a new tray! It's quite lovely. I like the piecrust rim. Is it antique? Where did you find it?"

"It was a kind of thank-you from the Bambas. I recommended Lori and Nick when the K Fund was looking for a couple to run the Nutcracker Inn. Let me read you the inscription."

It was: *For Qwill with the compliments of the Nutcracker Inn, where all the nuts go.*

Another vehicle pulled up to the kitchen door. The Rikers had come directly from the newspaper office. Mildred was the food editor; Arch was editor in chief and Qwilleran's lifelong friend. The two men had grown up together in Chicago and were secure enough in their friendship to taunt each other at the slightest provocation.

Mildred noticed the new tray on the bar. "It's charming! Where did you find it?"

"It was a gift. Glad you approve."

"It's not very old," said Arch, who considered himself an authority on antiques. "And it's only silver plate."

"It will do," Qwilleran said, "until you give me an eighteenth-century sterling tray for my birthday, which happens to be next month, in case you've forgotten."

When drinks were served and they moved to the deep-cushioned sofas around the fireplace, Arch proposed a toast: "To all who slave in the workplace from nine to five — and to those who only do two columns a week."

There was a quick retort from the author of the "Qwill Pen" column: "If I didn't write my thousand words every Tuesday and Friday, your circulation would drop fifty percent. By the way, do you have any news in tomorrow's newspaper?"

"Yes," Mildred said. "Good news on the food page! Derek Cuttlebrink's girlfriend and her two brothers in Chicago have purchased the Old Stone Mill, and it will have a new name, a new chef, and a new menu . . . *And* Derek will be the manager!"

The other three all talked at once. "Wonderful news!
... It's about time! ... There's nothing like having a
Chicago heiress for a girlfriend ... I wonder if he'll
stop growing now ... I remember him when he was
only a six-foot-four busboy and his ambition was to be
a cop ... The boy's got charisma! ... Wait till his
groupies hear the news! ... What will the new
restaurant be called?"

"The Grist Mill. That was its original purpose. The
farmers brought their wheat and corn to be ground
into flour."

Arch said, "I hope they get rid of the phony mill
wheel! The millstream dried up fifty years ago, they say,
and turning the wheel electrically was a harebrained
idea! The mechanical creaking and rumbling and
groaning gave the diners indigestion ... It drove me
crazy!"

"That's not hard to do," Qwilleran observed.

The Siamese had not been in evidence during the
conversation, and Mildred asked, "Where's sweet little
Yum Yum?"

She was under the sofa, advancing stealthily on
Arch's shoelaces.

"Where's King Koko?" he asked.

Koko heard his name and appeared from nowhere,
walking stiffly on his long, elegant legs. When he had
everyone's attention, he looked haughtily from one to
another, then turned and left the room.

"How's that for a royal put-down?" the editor remarked.

The party was in a jovial mood when they left for
dinner.

CHAPTER
THREE

The depressing old Pickax Hotel was now the upscale Mackintosh Inn — with a life-size portrait of Anne Mackintosh Qwilleran in the lobby, a new interior masterminded by Fran Brodie, and Mackintosh tartan seats in the main dining room. It was now called the Mackintosh Room, and a new chef had made it the finest restaurant in town.

The new maître d', being only five-foot-ten, lacked the panache of the six-foot-eight Derek Cuttlebrink, but he knew to seat Qwilleran's party at the best table.

They were a jovial foursome — middle-aged and comfortable with their lives and with each other. Yet, each had a history that could be told: Jim Qwilleran, after a failed marriage, had succumbed to alcoholism until a miracle got him back on track. Polly Duncan, widowed tragically at twenty-five, had never remarried. Mildred Hanstable Riker, stunned by a disastrous family situation, had survived with her warm heart and generous spirit intact. Arch Riker, after raising a family, had heard his first wife announce, "I'd rather be a single antique *dealer* than a married antique *collector*."

When they were seated and the menus were presented, Arch said, "I'd like a big steak."

His wife said sweetly, "Hon, you can have a big steak when you go to Tipsy's Tavern. Chef Wingo offers you a chance to expand your gustatory horizons. I think you'd like the garlic-and-black-pepper-marinated strip loin with caramelized onions and merlot-vinegar reduction."

Arch looked at the others helplessly. "What's Qwill having?"

His friend said, "Grilled venison tenderloin with smoked bacon, braised cabbage strudel, and Bing cherry demi-glaze."

Both women were having the seafood Napoleon with carrot gaufrettes and lemon buerre blanc sauce.

The first course was a butternut squash puree served in soup plates with a garnish of fresh blueberries.

Polly remarked, "Do I recognize Mildred's influence?"

"I told Wingo that blueberries are legendary in Moose County."

Qwilleran was alerted. He was collecting local legends for his book to be titled *Short & Tall Tales*. "Is it one for the book, Mildred? I'd like to tape it."

"Wonderful!" she said. "Bring your recorder to the opening of the stitchery exhibition on Sunday."

"What kind of stitchery?" Polly asked.

"Quilting. But not the kind of traditional bed quilts that I used to make. These are wall hangings, large and small, pictorial and geometric. We're calling it Touchy-Feely Art, and I'll tell you why. A number of years ago I was visiting an art museum in Chicago and trying to examine the brushwork on a certain painting. The security guard tapped me on the shoulder and said, "Stand back eighteen inches. Breathing on the paintings is prohibited." Well! The artwork we're showing on Sunday can be touched as well as breathed on. Even if you don't touch the wall hangings, you get a snuggly feeling just by looking at them."

"Interesting!" Qwilleran said, as he considered the ramifications of Touchy-Feely Art. "You'd better post signs WASH YOUR HANDS."

Then the entrees were served, and they talked about food for a while. The server had placed a small plate of lemon wedges in the middle of the table.

"What are those for?" Arch asked.

Mildred explained, "Chef Wingo believes a few drops of lemon add piquancy to any dish, hon."

"Qwill and I used to use it for invisible ink in secret correspondence . . . Remember that, Qwill?"

"Was it fourth grade?"

"I think it was fifth. Miss Getz was the teacher."

Polly said to Mildred, "Here we go again!" The two couples could never get together without another anecdote about rascally boyhood pranks. "Tell us about Miss Getz and the secret correspondence," she said coyly.

"Arch and I passed slips of blank paper back and forth in class, and she knew we were up to no good, but she never discovered the secret writing."

"The way it works," Arch explained, "you dip a cotton swab-stick in lemon juice and write on plain white paper. The writing isn't visible until you hold it up to a hot lamp bulb. But not too close."

24

Polly inquired, "Dare I ask what kind of messages you exchanged in the fourth grade?"

"Fifth," Arch corrected her. "There's a big difference."

Qwilleran smoothed his moustache, as he did when trying to recollect. "Well . . . there was a girl in our class called Pauline Pringle who had a bad case of acne. One day Arch slipped me a bit of paper. When I got it home and over a hot lightbulb, I laughed so hard — my mother thought I was having convulsions. It said: *Pauline Pimple likes you a lot.*"

Arch chuckled at the memory. The two women remained cool.

"The next day," Qwilleran went on, "I sent him a message about the teacher. Her face would get very red once in a while, and she'd mop her brow with a handkerchief. The message was: *Miss Getz sweats.*"

The women groaned. Polly was not attuned to schoolboy humor; and Mildred, having taught school for thirty years, empathized with the long-suffering Miss Getz. She said, "All you two miscreants deserve for dessert is lemon sorbet."

All four ordered Chef Wingo's famous blueberry cobbler, however. Arch wanted a dollop of ice cream on his; Polly asked for a smidgen of yogurt; Mildred thought she would like "just a tad" of whipped cream. The host took his neat.

But he asked, "Should I know what a tad is?"

"Halfway between a smidgen and a wee bit," Mildred informed him.

As they lingered over coffee, they discussed the Pickax Sesquicentennial celebration scheduled for the following year. Arch had attended the first meeting of the planning committee.

"I hate to tell you this," he said, "but they elected Hixie Rice as general chairman."

"Oh, no!" Mildred said.

"Oh, dear!" Polly muttered.

The promotion director of the *Moose County Something* was a clever idea-person with boundless energy and enthusiasm — and a record of disasters, through no fault of her own. There had been the Ice Festival that thawed out, the Mark Twain Festival canceled because of a murder, the cat contest that ended in a riot (of cat owners, not contestants), and more. The city was still wondering what to do with fifteen thousand polar-bear lapel buttons ordered for the Ice Festival.

Yet, Hixie always bounced back, entranced people with her optimism and creativity, and found herself elected to chair another fiasco.

The next day was a workday, so the party broke up early. For Qwilleran the evening was not over, however. At home he put a sheet of blank white paper in an envelope and addressed it to Arch, chuckling as he visualized his old friend's reaction. Though suspicious, his old friend would be unable to resist heating it over a lightbulb, and when he found it blank, Arch would lie awake all night plotting revenge.

The next day Qwilleran walked downtown to buy a *New York Times* and stopped at the design studio, a good place to get a cup of coffee and the latest news. Fran was back in town, he learned, but was taking a day off.

Her assistant was trying hard to be her boss's clone — in dress, manner, and hairstyle. But she was more talkative. Her name was Lucinda Holmes. She had a boyfriend named Dr Watson, she said with a giggle. He was a vet at the Whinny Hills Animal Clinic. They took care of her thoroughbred gelding and two English foxhounds. She loved riding to hounds. The clinic used to be the Thackeray clinic. It had changed a lot. It was very sad. Dr Thackeray was killed in an accident. There were rumors that it was suicide, or even murder.

Qwilleran asked, "Was he related to Fran's client?"

"He was her twin brother. She's a very interesting person. Fran took me out there on her first trip. We had to measure everything in the house. It's all being moved here, and floor plans have to be established before the moving men get here."

"So you're from Lockmaster! What brought you to Pickax?"

"I studied design at the Harrington School in Chicago and worked in Lockmaster for a while, but I wasn't learning anything. With Fran I learn how to present ideas to clients, how to listen to their own ideas, how to change their minds without offending them —"

A bell tinkled on the front door. Qwilleran drained his coffee cup and left Lucinda to practice her new skills on a client.

★　★　★

Back at the barn a red light was flashing on the answering machine, although Koko paid no attention to it. He had a way of screening calls and making a catly fuss when he deemed one important.

This one was from Fran Brodie, speaking in a throatily teasing way: "If you'll invite me over for a drink, I'll tell you all about Thelma Thackeray, but don't invite me to dinner; I'm dining with Dutch at the Palomino Paddock. I hope you know how to mix a marguerita. Just phone and leave a message: yes or no."

Qwilleran huffed into his moustache. Of course he could mix a marguerita — or anything else in the book. He had earned his way through college by tending bar.

He said to Yum Yum: "Guess who's coming over for a drink!" The fur on her neck was standing on end; she had recognized the voice on the machine.

CHAPTER
FOUR

The Qwilleran System of Weights and Measures was the topic of his next "Qwill Pen" column. He wrote:

How far is it to the nearest gas station? "Just a hop, skip, and a jump."

Where is the motel? "Down the road a piece."

Would you like more coffee? "Just a splash."

How about a drink of Scotch? "A wee dram."

How much hot sauce did you put in this soup? "Not much. Just a kachug."

How much longer do I have to wait to see the doctor? "He'll be with you in a jiffy."

How fast can you sew a button on? "In two shakes of a lamb's tail."

How much do you love me? "A whole bunch!"

When Qwilleran filed his copy with the managing editor, he said, "I owe you one, Junior; there really is a Thelma Thackeray. I'll take you to lunch at Rennie's."

"Super! I'm hungry! . . . Sit down. Be with you in a sec." The editor rushed from the office with proof sheets.

While pondering the difference between a sec and a jiffy, Qwilleran noticed a proof of the editorial page, with a letter from a reader who aired her views, forcefully and entertainingly.

TO THE EDITOR — My family attended the last open meeting of the county Board of Commissioners, so that my daughters could see how government works. The issue being addressed was the important one of zoning. May I respectfully inquire what language our esteemed board members were speaking? It sounded like Jabberwocky in *Through the Looking-Glass* — " 'Twas brillig, and the slithy toves did gyre and gimble in the wabe." We were not alone. Others in the audience, equally bewildered, gathered on the courthouse steps after the meeting and proposed a message to our elected officials: "All mimsy were the borogoves."

Mavis Adams
HBB&A

Junior returned, ready for a free lunch at his friend's expense, and they went to Rennie's coffee shop at the Mackintosh Inn. It was named for Charles Rennie Mackintosh and inspired by one of his tearooms in Glasgow: tables lacquered in bright blue and bright green, chairs with unusually high backs, napkins striped in black and white.

They ordered French dip sandwiches with fries and a Caesar salad.

Qwilleran asked, "Is there any news that's not fit to print?"

"We're all waiting for Thelma Thackeray. Would you like to interview her?"

"No thanks. It sounds like a story for Jill Handley."

The editor said, "We want to run a profile in depth. It will be good to have in the obit file. She's getting on in years."

"So are we all — except you, Junior. You still look like a summer intern."

"You don't have to rub it in, just because you're buying lunch."

"Have you heard what's going into the old opera house?"

"Someone said it's a new county jail."

"I was hoping for the world's largest emporium of used books. I miss Eddington's old place."

Junior said, "It's got to be an operation that requires a lot of parking space. They've torn down the storefront on both sides, and the lots are being paved."

"The plot thickens," Qwilleran said. "Shall we have dessert? The chocolate pecan pie sounds good."

They ordered the pie, and Junior said, "Are you still reading to your cats?"

"Absolutely! It sharpens their intellect. Since advocating it in my column, I've received scores of letters from readers, reporting striking results."

"Let's not overdo it," Junior warned. "The felines could take over the local government."

"Not a bad idea! We can start by packing the town council."

When the pie was served, they fell into a blissful silence for a while until Junior asked, "What are you reading to the cats now? Plato and Schopenhauer?"

"Noel Coward's biography. I sing some of the Coward songs. Koko likes the one about mad dogs and Englishmen."

The young editor never knew whether to take Qwilleran seriously or go along with the gag, so he concentrated on eating his pie.

Qwilleran had said "yes" to Fran Brodie's cavalier proposal and hoped he would not regret it. As four o'clock approached, he set up the work bar with tequila, lime, salt, the silver tray, and so forth. Yum Yum huddled apprehensively nearby. He told her, "Fran Brodie is coming for a drink. What do you want me to put in it?" She scampered away.

Fran was the picture of glamour — with her chic clothing, model's figure, artful grooming, and perfect legs. They were always enhanced by high-heeled strappy sandals, weather permitting. But the sophisticated designer and the sweet little female cat had been feuding from the beginning. Yum Yum was possessive about Qwilleran, and Fran came on strong, attracted by his large moustache, or large fortune, or both.

When he first arrived in Pickax, he gave her a key to his apartment to use in his absence. She came in with her installer to rearrange the furniture and hang the window blinds. Or she came alone to accessorize the rooms with framed prints, pillows, candles, and the like. She thought them important, and her client let her have her way.

The only accessory he owned was the very old Mackintosh crest in wrought iron, said to come from a Scottish castle. It was leaning against the wall in the hallway, and she thought it would do nicely as camouflage for an ugly old radiator. While rolling it into the living room like a hoop, she accidentally rolled the fifty-pound artifact over her sandaled foot. She claimed that Yum Yum had darted out from nowhere and made her do it. A few weeks in a surgical boot cooled her ardor for the Klingenschoen heir. He had never liked sexually aggressive women anyway, preferring to do the pursuing himself. Whether or not Yum Yum had caused the accident was a moot point, but Fran was forever paranoid about female cats.

Her first words, when she arrived for her marguerita, were "Where is she?"

"They're both in the gazebo," he said.

"You have a new silver tray! It's not what I would have chosen for this environment, but it's nice — not good, but nice."

She was looking stunning in a periwinkle silk suit and new hair color, and high-heeled strappy shoes — all chosen, no doubt, for her dinner date with . . . "Dutch".

Qwilleran said, "You're looking spiffy, in spite of your arduous trip . . . Let's sit in the living room."

She sank into one of the deep-cushioned sofas and looked critically at the fireplace cube. Its face — above and on both sides of the fireplace — was covered with adjustable bookshelves. "Do you really need to have those shelves on this side of the cube?" she asked.

"I'm running out of wall space," he said as he raised his glass. "Cheers!"

"Cheers! . . . What are you drinking?"

"The new Qwilleran cocktail . . . Recipe is being patented."

His guest still stared at the wall of books. "Is it a good idea to have books above a fireplace? I should think the heat would be bad for the bindings. If you could possibly remove them, I could get you a large sculptural wall accent —"

"Too bad I gave the Mackintosh crest to the inn," he said, slyly.

Fran changed the subject abruptly. "You met my new assistant yesterday. Did she tell you anything?"

"Yes, she seems to be interested in dogs and horses."

"I mean, did she tell you anything about Thelma Thackeray?"

"She simply said she was interesting."

"She's that, all right," Fran agreed. "And a good client! She knows what she likes, is open to suggestions, makes quick decisions, and doesn't change her mind. She's been in the business world for almost fifty years, and it shows! Also, she wants the very best and is willing to pay for it." The marguerita was working its spell. Fran was less edgy; she was willing to talk.

"What kind of career did she have in California?"

"She started with a sandwich shop, then a good restaurant, and then a private dinner club. It's her

34

strong personality, I think, that has made her a success. Friends and customers gave her a smashing farewell party."

"Why did she decide to come back to Moose County — of all places?"

"Her only living relative is here, and you know how it is: People tend to get sentimental about family as they grow older."

Fran held out her glass for a refill and kicked off her shoes. "You really know how to mix margueritas, Qwill!"

He served another drink. "When does Madame Thackeray arrive?"

"It's all orchestrated. She left before the movers arrived, and she'll arrive after they've delivered. Everything will be unpacked at this end."

"How much staff does she have?"

"Secretary, housekeeper, and driver," Fran said slyly, waiting for a reaction. Then she added, "They're all the same person — more of a companion — a woman half her age, who's really devoted to Thelma."

Qwilleran said, "I could use one of those when I'm her age. How old is she?"

"Eighty-two, but she certainly doesn't look it!"

"Face-lift?" he inquired.

"That's another terrific thing about Thelma. She eats right, exercises, and gives herself a daily face-lift with the electromagnetic rays from her fingertips . . . Perhaps I shouldn't be telling all this — to the media."

"One question," Qwilleran said. "Why did she choose to buy property on Pleasant Street?"

"She remembered it from her childhood, when her father — who was a potato farmer — used to drive the family into town in his Model T — to see movies. As an extra treat he also drove up and down Pleasant Street. To those kids it was like Grimms' fairy tales. They were like huge gingerbread houses decorated with white frosting in fancy scrolls. So when she called a realtor here and learned that one of the storybook houses was listed for sale, she flipped!"

"Do you know Mavis Adams, the attorney?" she asked abruptly.

"I know she's the new "A" in HBB&A. We've met briefly."

"The realtor recommended her to handle legal details of the property transfer. Also, Thelma will have to file a new will in this state . . . Mavis thinks the residents of Pleasant Street should give a reception to welcome Thelma."

"Friendly idea," Qwilleran said. "Since half the families on the street are Scottish, you could hold it at the Scottish lodge hall."

Fran gave him a sly glance. "We hoped you'd let us use your barn."

"Hmmm," he mused. "That's something to think about!"

"Think fast. It's to be a week from Sunday. Robin-O'Dell will do the catering, and Burgess Campbell will take care of expenses. The Scots will be in Highland attire, which makes for a gala mood."

"Well . . . since you're working on a short deadline . . . I'll say yes." Qwilleran liked any excuse to wear his Highland kit.

"Everyone will be delighted, and Thelma will be terribly impressed." Fran was putting on her shoes.

"Before you leave, let me bring in Yum Yum," Qwilleran said. "You two rational females should bury the hatchet."

"No, no! She'll nip my nylons even if she doesn't break my foot!"

He accompanied her to the barnyard and noted that she was driving a new car — a luxury model. The Thackeray assignment must have been lucrative.

Before stepping into the car, she hesitated and then said, "As a favor to me, Qwill, would you let me supply an artwork to hang over your fireplace, replacing the bookshelves, just temporarily? Thelma knows I did the interior of the barn, and I want it to look its best."

"I'll take it under advisement," he said gravely. He felt about his books the way parents feel about their children.

When he brought them in from the gazebo and watched Koko gobbling his dinner and Yum Yum nibbling daintily, he thought, How could this sweet little creature be accused of nipping nylons?

Later, he asked Polly on the phone, "Does Catta ever nip women's nylons?"

"No. Why do you ask?"

"I've heard that some female cats have a nylon fetish."

37

He was careful not to mention Fran's visit. Polly disliked her flip manner and such gaucheries as kicking off her shoes when offered a second drink. Polly called the gesture "just too cute."

So Qwilleran told her only that the pleasant people on Pleasant Street wanted to borrow the barn for a reception welcoming Thelma. "It'll be a week from Sunday. Highland dress is suggested, since half the residents are Scots."

"Lovely!" she said. "Am I invited? I'll wear my clan sash, pinned on the shoulder with a cairngorm."

"You're not only invited; you're in charge of background music — preferably light classics that make people feel good but aren't too boringly familiar."

"I have just the thing! The piano pieces of Sibelius. They'll be thrilling on your stereo system."

Then he told her he was thinking of removing the books over the fireplace and replacing them with artwork.

She approved. "I've always thought that was a risky place for book bindings. The heat could dry them out, you know. You might find a suitable wall hanging at the Art Center Sunday."

Having Polly in accord with his two forthcoming projects, he tackled the preparations with a modicum of enthusiasm.

Qwilleran was inept at household maintenance chores. He worked with words and believed that carpenters should work with hammers, plumbers with wrenches, and painters with brushes. Whenever he had attempted a simple do-it-yourself project, the Siamese sensed the gravity of the occasion and watched with apprehension. He said to them, "Keep your toes crossed and if I fall off the ladder, call 911."

The job called for removing the books, the shelving, the brackets that held the shelves, and the metal strips that supported the brackets, leaving several large screwholes in the wall. He seemed to remember that such holes could be filled with toothpaste, but the wall was white, and his current toothpaste was green. The obvious solution was to buy a wall hanging large enough to cover the blemishes. It would require an artwork at least five feet wide and three feet high.

CHAPTER
FIVE

In the late nineteenth century the octagonal apple barn had presided over one of the strip farms of the period — almost a half mile long, but narrow. A wagon trail ran its length. Now it was a single-lane country road, seldom used for vehicular traffic. Qwilleran used it to walk from the barn to his rural mailbox and newspaper sleeve on the back road and to the Art Center at the far end.

On Sunday Qwilleran and Polly walked down the lane to the Touchy-Feely Exhibition — he with a tape measure in his pocket.

On the way down, she asked, "Did I tell you that the library has had a run on novels by William Makepeace Thackeray?"

His acerbic reply: "Only Moose County could put two and two together and get seventeen . . . Did you find out anything about his middle name?"

"Not a clue! . . . I had an uncle Makemoney — at least, that's what I called him. He was always talking about making money! My father, who was very precise about language, said you can earn money, invest money, inherit money, save money, and lose money but you cannot make money. You would have liked my father, Qwill, and he would have approved of you."

"My loss," he murmured.

The skeletons of blighted apple trees had been replaced by a garden that attracted birds, another designed for butterflies, and reforestation with hardwoods and evergreens.

The Art Center at the end of the lane resembled a rustic residence, and that was what it was originally intended to be. Now it was a complex of exhibition halls, studios, and classrooms. The new show featured stitchery inspired by great artists. There were sunflowers (Van Gogh), apples (Cézanne), super-flowers (O'Keeffe), trompe l'oeil (Harnett), and so forth.

For himself he found an abstraction inspired by Feininger — an explosion of color, leading the eye into the distance. And it was the right size! A "sold" sticker was affixed. According to gallery policy, purchased artworks had to remain in the exhibition until the end of the month. He consulted the manager about the forthcoming reception.

"No problem! We'll notify the artist, and she'll be flattered to have her work on display in your fabulous barn."

Mildred Riker was there, ready to recount the blueberry legend of Moose County, and they went into a vacant studio to do the taping.

"Arch kids me about throwing a handful of blueberries into everything," she said, "but they're part of Moose County's history."

On the desk was a metal scoop about ten inches wide, with about thirty metal prongs. Qwilleran said, "What's that? It would be good for policing a cat's commode."

Stifling a giggle, Mildred said, "That's a blueberry rake used in harvesting."

He turned on the recorder, and the following tale was later transcribed:

THE INCREDIBLE
MOOSE COUNTY BLUEBERRIES

Long before we knew about antioxidants and bioflavonoids, blueberries were doing their thing; Mother Nature had made them good-for-you as well as good-to-eat. In the seventeenth century French explorers reported that native Americans used wild blueberries as food and medicine.

In the nineteenth century my great-grandfather, Elias King, came to Moose County from Maine to work as a lumberjack and save up to buy a farm. His diary is preserved in the historical collection at the public library.

He wrote that the woods were full of wild blueberries, called bilberries. The lumberjacks ate them by the handful. They were like candy — after the lumber-camp diet of beans and salt pork.

Eventually he had saved enough to buy farmland at the north edge of what is now Pickax. The land was well endowed with wild blueberries — low-growing shrubs that crept across the property as if they owned it.

When my grandfather, Matthew King, inherited the farm, he claimed that blueberries occupied more acreage than did corn and potatoes. He said, "Wild blueberries can't be cultivated, but they can't be killed, either." So he gave the berries away to anyone who cared to pick them. Grandma King said she lay awake nights, thinking of ways to use them in family meals: a handful of blueberries here, a handful of blueberries there. The perfect blueberry pie recipe that she masterminded is in my security box at the bank.

By the time my father inherited the property, the family was involved in producing, packaging, marketing, and shipping blueberry products. He was jocularly called the Blueberry King, and friends launched a frivolous campaign to change the name of the area to Blueberry County. Their slogan: "When was the last time you saw a Moose?"

Finally my brothers and I were bequeathed the blueberry empire, but we were interested in careers of our own. We sold out to the large Toodle family, who developed the property in various ways, including a supermarket with extensive parking and loading facilities. They carry excellent produce from all parts of the country. Included are the large cultivated berries that I put in muffins, pancakes, soups, salads, stews, and Grandma King's blueberry pie. Considering my blueberry heritage, it seems ironic that I now buy the berries in eight-ounce boxes . . . No matter. There is a postscript to the tale.

The supermarket has had constant trouble with the parking lot. Asphalt buckled. Concrete cracked. One day Grandma Toodle showed me the latest damage. Shrubs were pushing up in the wide cracks.

"What do you think they are?" she asked.

"I know what they are!" I said. "Nothing can stop the incredible Moose County blueberries."

Qwilleran turned off the recorder and said, "Mildred, millions of people wouldn't believe that blueberries could wreck a parking lot . . . but I do!"

On Monday morning Koko was huddled over his plate, concentrating on his food, when he suddenly turned his head to the side and listened for a few seconds before returning his attention to the business at hand. Moments later, he turned again, and the telephone rang.

It was a welcome call from Thornton Haggis, the Art Center's volunteer man-of-all-work. He said, "Mildred told me yesterday that you bought a wall hanging and it's okay to take it before the show ends. I could drive it up there and hang it for you right now."

Qwilleran said, "Best news I've had since Amanda was elected mayor. I have a stepladder. What else do you need?"

"Nothing. I have all the tools and know all the tricks for hanging textiles."

"Then come along. I'll start the coffeemaker."

The Siamese were excited when they saw the stepladder come out of the broom closet, and saw a car moving up the lane that seldom knew traffic, and saw a white-haired man approaching the barn with a big roll of something under his arm.

"Where do we hang it?" were Thornton's first words.

"Above the fireplace, covering the holes."

"It won't cover! It's a vertical."

"Just hang it horizontally."

The expert unrolled the hanging on the floor and studied it from all angles. "Why not?" was his decision. "But we won't tell the artist."

After the deed was done and the result admired, the men sat at the snack bar for coffee and some sweet rolls from the freezer.

"Terrific rolls! Where'd you get them?" Thornton asked.

"From a woman in Fishport who sells home-bakes."

"I know her. She and her husband reported a missing person last summer and got all that unfavorable publicity. A shame! Nice folks, the Hawleys. He's a commercial fisherman, semi-retired."

Thornton knew everyone in the county, past and present.

They talked about the Sesquicentennial and the Haggis Monument Works, purveyor of gravestones for a century and a half.

"My forebears chiseled some outlandish inscriptions in the early days, and I photograph them whenever I find them."

"You should write a book," Qwilleran suggested. "I'm sure the K Fund would publish it. I'll buy the first copy."

"Do you think the restored opera house has anything to do with the Sesquicentennial, Qwill? I have a hunch it's going to be the big event of the celebration, and that's why they're being so secretive."

If so, Qwilleran thought, and if it was Hixie's idea, something dire will happen! Not wanting to be a doom-sayer, he changed the subject casually after a brief pause: "Where do you get your hair cut, Thorn?"

"When my wife lets me get it cut, I go to Bob the Barber, which isn't very often; she likes the Zulu look."

Bob the Barber did business in a curious old building on Main Street. It was set back a few feet from its neighbors, and steps led down from the sidewalk to a small patio at basement level. Here there was a park bench, a potted tree, and an old revolving barber pole. One could look through a large window and see how many customers were waiting.

Qwilleran said, "You don't often see a barber pole anymore, especially one that revolves. I've often wondered about the significance of the spiral red-and-white pole."

Thornton was a history buff and the right one to ask. He said, "In the Middle Ages there were barber-surgeons who did bloodletting with leeches. They hung bandages on a pole outside their shop to advertise the services. The colors on the barber pole that evolved were red for blood, white for bandages, blue for veins."

"Sorry I asked," Qwilleran said.

A haircut was on his schedule for Monday, a day that was usually not busy. When he walked down the steps to the barbershop, he discovered that other customers had the same idea. Through the large window he could see both barber chairs occupied and several customers waiting in the row of folding chairs against the wall. A man in overalls, a feed cap, and field boots was leaving the shop. He said, "Can't wait . . . too slow. Young Bob broke his thumb."

"Cutting hair?" Qwilleran asked.

He could see Old Bob working at the first chair and Young Bob, with a splint on his left hand, at the second chair.

"Playin' softball," the farmer said. "He can wiggle his fingers some, but . . . too slow . . . too slow. Ain't got time."

Among those who had time to wait were an agricultural agent, a storekeeper, and a lecturer at the community college. Burgess Campbell, blind from birth, was accompanied by his guide dog, Alexander.

The two men played their usual charade.

Qwilleran said, "Professor Moriarty! Are you here for a haircut or a bloodletting?"

"My friend Sherlock!" he replied. "Did you bring your violin?"

"Shouldn't you be in the lecture hall, professor?"

"Not until one o'clock. When are you going to audit one of my lectures?"

"What's this week's topic?"

"Geopolitical Machinations in the Nineteenth Century."

"I'll wait till next week," Qwilleran said.

Old Bob whipped the sheet off his customer and said, "Either of you two jokers ready to be clipped?"

Qwilleran said to Burgess, "You go first. I want to look at the bulletin board."

"All I need is a trim. You can have the chair in . . . *two shakes of a lamb's tail*." His emphasis on the last phrase was a pointed reference to the "Qwill Pen."

There was a wall of cork near the entrance, where customers were welcome to post their business cards: Bill's Bump Shop, Main Street Flowers, Tipsy's Tavern, and the like. But interspersed with the legitimate cards were computer printouts that local wags contributed:

TRAFFIC TICKETS FIXED — CHEAP

FALSE IDS — WHILE U WAIT

TAX-EVASION SERVICE — TOP-QUALITY ADVICE

Qwilleran asked the head barber, "Do the police ever raid this joint?"

"When Andy Brodie comes in for a clip, he heads straight for the board and laughs his head off," said Old Bob.

After Qwilleran's session in the barber chair, he found Burgess and Alexander waiting for him on the patio.

"Got a minute to sit down, Qwill? I want to thank you for letting us have the reception in your barn."

"My pleasure. But you've never visited the barn, and — as the host of the occasion — you should drop in and get the lay of the land."

"Good idea! I can have a student driver take me over there any afternoon after three o'clock."

"I assume you refer to an MCCC student who drives — and not a kid who's learning to operate a vehicle."

Burgess laughed heartily ... and an appointment was made.

CHAPTER
SIX

Qwilleran had mixed feelings about Pleasant Street. Residents included some of his best friends, important in the community and known for intelligence and taste. They lived in large houses set well apart on one-acre lots — frame houses — painted white and lavished with white jigsaw ornamentation.

To Qwilleran, with his eye for contemporary, they looked like a collection of wedding cakes! Yet, the street had been photographed often and featured in national magazines as a fine example of Carpenter Gothic.

They had been built by the Campbells in the nineteenth century, and while the residents owned their dwellings, Burgess Campbell owned the land. That fact gave him a baronial interest in the neighborhood and the well-being of its occupants.

Now, Qwilleran felt it behooved him to take a closer look at Pleasant Street. He would bike, pedaling his vintage British Silverlight. With his slick red-and-yellow bike suit, yellow bubble helmet, sun goggles, and oversize moustache, he had been known to stop traffic on Main Street. (On one occasion a car back-ended another at a traffic light.) So he approached Pleasant Street via the back road.

It was a cul-de-sac, with a landscaped island at the end for a turnaround. The five houses on each side had broad lawns, and the serenity of the scene was enhanced by the fact that there was no curb-parking. Each dwelling had a side-drive with garage and visitor parking in the rear. There was a Wednesday-morning quiet: children at school, adults at work or doing errands or volunteer work. Others would be pursuing their hobbies. A contralto could be heard doing vocal exercises. The distant whine of a table saw meant that the woodworker was making a Shaker table.

Qwilleran biked twice up and down the street then stopped at the entrance to appraise the whole. No two houses were alike, yet they all had a vertical silhouette. There were tall narrow windows and doors, steeply pitched roofs over a third floor. Some had turrets. All had a wealth of ornamentation along roof lines, balcony railings, atop doors and windows.

Before leaving the scene he braked his bike and scanned the streetscape through squinted eyes. He was reluctant to admit that it had a kind of enchantment, like an illustrated edition of a book of fairy tales. Its residents included businessmen, two doctors, a college lecturer, an attorney, a professional astrologer, a musician, and an artist! Perhaps Burgess could explain the lure of Pleasant Street.

Qwilleran had time to take a quick shower, drop some crunchies into the plate on the kitchen floor, and wolf down a ham sandwich before his appointment with Burgess. Then, a few minutes before three o'clock,

Koko rushed to the kitchen window. He sensed that a car was turning off Main Street, crossing the theatre parking lot, and meandering through the woods to the barn.

Qwilleran went out to meet it and saw the two front doors fly open. A dog jumped out the passenger door, followed by a man in lecture-hall tweeds. The driver, in jeans and T-shirt, emerged with an expression of rapt wonder.

"Hey, man! That's some kinda barn!!"

Burgess said, "Qwill, this is Henry Ennis, chauffeur par excellence. Hank, you can pick me up at four o'clock."

"Make it four-thirty," Qwilleran suggested.

The driver said, "If you want me earlier, call the library. I'll be studying there."

As he drove away, Burgess explained, "Hank is a scholarship student from Sawdust City. I reserve my second floor as a hostel for MCCC students without cars, who can't go home every night."

Burgess employed students part-time to read aloud — from research material, the *New York Times*, and student papers for grading.

Qwilleran said, "Okay! The tour starts here . . . On Sunday night parking will have to be here in the barnyard, and space is limited. So guests should be instructed to car-pool."

Burgess made a note of it on a small recorder.

"Actually, this is the kitchen door, so someone will have to direct them around the barn to the front entrance. It's a stone path, so women will find it kind to their high heels. I'm assuming it will be a dressy occasion . . . I suggest that guests assemble in the bird garden before going indoors. There are stone benches and flowering shrubs, and I think we can get Andy Brodie to play the bagpipe for a half hour."

They went indoors, and Qwilleran conducted them through the large foyer, where the receiving line would be stationed . . . through the dining room, where Robin-O'Dell would have the refreshment table set up . . . past the snack bar with its four stools for guests who like to sit and lean on their elbows . . . through the library with its comfortable seating . . . and into the living room with its large sofas.

Burgess asked, "Where are the cats? I can tell they're here — by the way Alexander is breathing."

Qwilleran said, "They're on the rafters, which are forty feet overhead. They're watching every move we make."

When all the decisions were made, and all the notes were recorded, they sat at the snack bar for cold drinks, and another story was taped for *Short & Tall Tales*.

HOW PLEASANT STREET GOT ITS NAME

In the nineteenth century my ancestors were shipbuilders in Scotland — in the famous river Clyde at Glasgow. When opportunity beckoned from the New World, my great-grandfather, Angus, came here with a team of ships' carpenters considered the best anywhere. They started a shipyard at Purple Point, where they built four-masted wooden schooners, using Moose

County's hundred-and-twenty-foot pine trees as masts. These were the "tall ships" that brought goods and supplies to the settlers and shipped out cargoes of coal, lumber, and stone.

Then came the New Technology! The wireless telegraph was in; the Pony Express was out. Railroads and steamboats were in; four-masted schooners were out. In his diary Angus said it was like a knife in the heart to see a tall ship stripped down to make a barge for towing coal. There was no work for his carpenters to do, and their fine skills were wasted.

Then a "still small voice" told him to build houses! It was the voice of his wife, Anne, a canny Scotswoman. She said, "John, build houses as romantic as the tall ships — and as fine!"

She was right! The New Technology had produced a class of young upwardly mobile achievers who wanted the good life. Not for them the stodgy stone mansions built by conspicuously rich mining tycoons and lumber barons! They wanted something romantic!

So Angus bought acreage at the south edge of Pickax and built ten fine houses, each on one-acre plots. Although no two were alike, their massing followed the elongated vertical architecture called Gothic Revival, and the abundance of scroll trim was the last word in Carpenter Gothic.

And here is something not generally known: The vertical board-and-batten siding was painted in the colors that delighted young Victorians: honey, cocoa, rust, jade, or periwinkle; against this background, the white scroll trim had a lacy look.

Today we paint them all-white, giving rise to the "wedding cake" sobriquet.

When the time came to put up sign boards, Angus was at a loss for a street name. He said, "I don't want anything personal like Campbell or Glasgow . . . or anything sobersides or high-sounding . . . just something pleasant."

And Great-Grandma Anne said with sweet feminine logic: "Call it Pleasant Street."

"And folks have lived there happily ever after," Qwilleran said as he turned off the recorder. "I don't even know who my grandparents were, so I'm envious of a fourth-generation native."

"I wanted to make it five generations," Burgess said, "but it didn't work out. I grew up with the girl next door and we were good friends. I always thought we'd marry some day, but she went away to college and never came back. Now she has three kids that should have been mine. But her parents still treat me like a son-in-law. And I treat students who lodge with me on the second floor with fatherly concern."

Qwilleran said, "They're very lucky! I hope they all turn out to be a credit to you . . . and how do you feel about the people who own the houses on your land?"

"We work together to keep Pleasant Street pleasant, solve problems, and so forth."

"Has the California contingent arrived?" Qwilleran asked casually.

"They're due this afternoon," Burgess said. "My housekeeper, Mrs Richards, periodically goes over with coffee and cookies — in the guise of neighborliness but actually because she and I are burning with curiosity. The moving van arrived Monday. Since then, Fran's helpers have worked around the clock, unpacking and getting everything settled. The house looks as if they had lived there for weeks!"

"One question," Qwilleran asked. "Do you know anything about the Thackeray family?"

"I certainly do!" was the prompt answer. "Thelma's father was a potato farmer who struck oil — as the saying goes — during Prohibition. Her brother was a veterinarian who believed in holistic medicine, and the Thackeray Clinic was one of the finest in this part of the country. I took Alexander to him for regular checkups. Dr Thurston's love of animals was such that they looked forward to visiting him. He was healthy and an outdoorsman and should have lived another ten years at least, but he fell to his death while hiking alone on the rim of the Black Creek Gorge. Tragic! The pity of it is: There are nasty rumors in circulation — which I prefer not to repeat."

A horn sounded in the barnyard, and Qwilleran walked with his visitors to the car. "One question, Burgess. Fran said the reception was for adults only —"

"Ah, yes! There'll be a party at the Adams house for the six kids in the neighborhood, ages seven to ten. Mavis's two teen daughters will supervise. They're accustomed to working with youngsters. They tell me there'll be games with prizes, movies — such as

56

Disney's *Lady and the Tramp* and/or *The Incredible Journey*. Music will be Sixties-style. Refreshment — four kinds of pizza and make-it-yourself sundaes . . . The Adams girls are very well organized and very responsible . . . And I forgot — favors to take home. Chocolate brownies."

Qwilleran said, "Sounds better than the champagne reception."

Alexander gently nudged Burgess toward the passenger door of the car, and they drove away.

The next evening Qwilleran and Polly would be dining at the newly named, newly decorated Grist Mill. She always dressed carefully for such occasions and had phoned the restaurant to inquire about the color scheme. It was jade green. So she would wear her dusty rose suit.

She reported this vital information to Qwilleran during their nightly phone-chat.

By a strange coincidence he was writing a think piece on green for his next "Qwill Pen" column. He boasted that he could take any noun or adjective and write a thousand words about it. Now the word was *green*. First . . . he made notes:

- It's the fourth color in the spectrum: red, orange, yellow, GREEN, blue, violet. Why is it more talked about than other colors?
- In big-city phone directories there are hundreds of Greens — and a few Greenes.

- Yet, there has never been a President Green in the White House.
- Why is blue more popular in clothing and the home? How do you feel about green jeans?
- Why does Santa wear red instead of green?
- Why do crazy kids dye their hair green?
- Green trees fight pollution. Green veggies are good for you.
- Green rhymes with mean. Monsters are green eyed. Nobody likes to be called a greenhorn. "It's not easy being green," according to the song.
- We have green alligators, green snakes, and green grasshoppers. Why no animals with green fur?

"Yow!" came an indignant comment. It was a reminder that it was eleven o'clock and time for a bedtime snack.

CHAPTER
SEVEN

In dressing for dinner at the Grist Mill, Qwilleran had chosen light olive-green slacks and a lighter olive-green shirt to wear with his tan blazer, and he had gone to Scottie's Men's Store for a deeper olive-green tie with a tan motif. His interest in coordination amazed Arch Riker, who had known him in his earlier, or "slob," period. Now Qwilleran had Polly to please, a host of admirers to impress, and a little money to spend.

Driving to the Grist Mill, they talked about the new animal-welfare project being launched in Moose County. The attorney, Mavis Adams, was spearheading it. It was being called the Kit Kat Agenda.

Polly said, "Its thrust is to stop the euthanasia of unwanted kittens. They're going to stage a show to raise funds."

"Mavis writes clever letters to the editor," he said.

"She lives on Pleasant Street."

"I wonder how Thelma will fit into the neighborhood?"

Polly said, "Guess who came into my office today? Thelma Thackeray's assistant! She took out library cards for both of them and then came to my office to introduce herself and make an offer. She was

conservatively dressed, soft-spoken, very nice —
fortyish, I guess — and obviously devoted to her boss."

"What was the offer?"

"Well, Thelma has a collection of autographed
photos of old movie stars that she'll lend us for an
exhibit. I assured her that we have a locked case for
such exhibits. Clark Gable, Mae West, John Wayne, Joan
Crawford, etc. — isn't that exciting?"

"If you say so," he said.

"There's even a signed print of a photo that
appeared on the cover of *Time* magazine: Hedda
Hopper wearing a hat made of a typewriter, a
microphone, and a script."

Before Qwilleran could react, they arrived at the
Grist Mill. "You must tell me more later," he said.

It was the same ancient stone mill with cavernous
interior and exposed timbers, but color had been
added: jade green table linens and carpet in a darker
shade of jade green. And the rough stone wall was hung
with farm implements of the nineteenth century.

They were greeted in the lobby by Elizabeth Hart,
one of the three owners, wearing a silk coolie suit in
jade green. Towering over the maître d's station was the
six-foot-eight Derek Cuttlebrink. He showed them to a
choice table — under a murderous-looking scythe.

Qwilleran said, "I hope that thing is securely
attached to the wall."

Polly said, "You have a fortune invested in antique
farm equipment!"

In a lowered voice Derek said, "Don't let on that I
told you, but Liz got them from Hollywood — props

from a movie." Then he added, "One dry sherry and one Qwilleran cocktail?"

The tables were filling rapidly with guests excited about the restaurant's opening. The menu was new and appetizing. Polly ordered three small courses: Mushroom bisque, deviled crab en coquille, and a Cobb salad. Qwilleran ordered minestrone, oysters Rockefeller, and the surf-and-turf special, and no salad. Polly said, "If Mildred were here, she'd make you eat some leafy greens."

Suddenly a hush fell on the room. Everyone looked toward the entrance. "What happened?" asked Qwilleran, who had his back to the door.

The young woman serving them exclaimed, "It's HER!" and she rushed to the kitchen.

Polly, facing the scene of the action, said, "Party of three . . . Thelma has a commanding appearance . . . One is the assistant who came to my office . . . There's a man with them . . . Everyone's gawking."

The hush gave way to an excited babble of voices.

"Thelma," she went on, "is wearing a pearl gray suit and small matching hat and jeweled lapel pin . . . She's doing the ordering. They're having champagne . . . The man is about forty. Looks like one of those 'snappy dressers' from Lockmaster . . . Is he her only living relative?"

Qwilleran said, "I believe the house she bought is the one you inherited — one of the best on Pleasant Street."

"Yes. I was terribly tempted to keep it and live there. I'm glad you talked me out of it, dear. It would have been too much property to care for, considering the demands of my job . . . But the people who live on Pleasant Street are so congenial! I think there's something psychological about the name of the street. The Campbells have always kept title to the land, and the neighborhood is like a dukedom. Did you know that Burgess is affectionately called 'Duke' by the residents?"

Polly ordered a small sorbet for dessert and watched without envy as Qwilleran consumed a large serving of cinnamon bread pudding with butterscotch sauce.

Thelma's party was still there when they left. In the lobby Polly excused herself, and Qwilleran sauntered to the maître d's desk. "Derek, are your responsibilities here going to interfere with your folksinging and theatre club productions?"

"Liz says we can work something out. I'm gonna be in the Kit Kat Revue."

"Sounds like a nightclub in an old musical comedy."

"It's a fund-raiser for an animal welfare project, and I wondered if you could write some lyrics about unwanted kittens. Sort of a tearjerker."

It was the kind of challenge he relished. He said, "You mean . . . something like . . . 'Frankie and Johnny were kittens . . . Lordy! How they could cry! . . . They sat in a cage for adoption . . . But people just passed 'em by . . . We done 'em wrong . . . We done 'em wrong!' "

"Super! Could you write a couple of more verses, Qwill?"

"I guess so. But if you let anyone know I'm writing your lyrics, you'll be singing without an Adam's apple!"

At that moment Polly joined them, and Derek said, "Enjoy your dinner, Mrs Duncan? I was just telling Mr Q that our chef trained in Singapore."

"Oh, really!" she said. "Elizabeth said he was from New Jersey."

"Well . . . His basic training was in Singapore," Derek said with the aplomb of one who is a frequent fibber.

On the way home Polly said, "I asked Elizabeth about the lapel pin Thelma was wearing. She said it's a parrot pavéd with emeralds and rubies, with a diamond eye, and she was also wearing a matching bracelet. Even Elizabeth was impressed!"

Qwilleran asked, "Do you know anything about the Kit Kat Revue?"

"Only that it's a fund-raiser for Mavis Adams's new animal rescue project. She'll be at the reception Sunday. I wonder what Thelma will wear? All those kilts and sashes will be strong competition."

Qwilleran said, "Fran Brodie will advise her. Fran is making herself indispensable."

"I suppose the man at Thelma's table was her nephew. He was quite good-looking and he was being terribly charming," Polly reported.

"As the only living relative of a rich octogenarian, it behooves him to be terribly charming."

"Oh, Quill! You're being so cynical!"

★ ★ ★

Cynical or not, he found his moustache bristling — even more so when a motorcycle messenger delivered an envelope Friday morning. A computer-printed invitation: "Please join us in honoring our California friends at a light repast directly after the reception — in the ballroom of the Mackintosh Inn. Southwest cuisine." It was signed by Richard Thackeray with no RSVP requested. It was assumed, innocently or haughtily, that everyone would be eager to attend.

The handwriting on the envelope was Fran's. So was the wording of the invitation, although the idea must have been Richard's. A supper riding piggyback on a reception would not occur to Fran. Qwilleran knew her well enough for that. She was humoring Richard — for whatever reason. (He could think of several.)

Nevertheless, he phoned Polly at the library to report the invitation. "It means you'll be getting home two or three hours later than expected. You might like to clear it with Brutus and Catta."

"Oh! Didn't I tell you? I have an automatic feeder with a timer, and it works very well. Wetherby Goode saw the item in a catalogue and bought one for each of us." The WPKX meteorologist (real name Joe Bunker) was a neighbor of Polly's and had a cat named Jet Stream. "Why don't you order one, Qwill? I'll get the phone number for you."

"Thanks, but I doubt whether Koko would approve. It might work for Yum Yum, but Koko likes to know the hand that feeds him."

Next, Qwilleran finished "All About Green" and walked downtown to file his copy before deadline.

Junior Goodwinter gave it an editor's quick scan and said, "You always boast, Qwill, that you can write a thousand words about nothing, and — by golly! — you've finally proved it!"

With equal mockery Qwilleran retorted, "What have you got on the front page today — if anything?"

"Thelma and her parrots," the managing editor replied. "Great photo by Bushy, but the text sounds like a press release. It'll be handy to have in the obit file; that's the best I can say for it. You should have written it, Qwill."

"I always thought Jill was a good writer."

"Yeah, but she's accustomed to interviewing locals. She allowed herself to be buffaloed by a celebrity. I had a professor in J school who hammered it into our skulls: *Don't be a respecter of persons!*"

"Not bad advice," Qwilleran agreed.

"On my first assignment I was supposed to interview a Very Important Person. The ignoramus sidestepped my questions and read a prepared speech — until I said, 'Excuse me, sir, may I ask a simple question?' He listened to it and said coldly, 'You should know the answer to that one.' I said respectfully, 'Yes, sir, but I want to know if you do.' Wow! Was I taking a chance, but it worked, and I got a good interview."

Qwilleran nodded with understanding. Junior had a handicap — an appearance of eternal youth. He looked like a high-school sophomore when he was in college, and now — as managing editor of a newspaper and father of two — he still looked fifteen.

★ ★ ★

When Qwilleran arrived home, Koko let him know there was a message on the answering machine: "This is Celia, Chief. We're catering your party on Sunday. Okay if I run over this afternoon to check the facilities and see what has to be done?"

Koko recognized the voice, despite the electronic distortion. It was the woman who brought them meat loaf. He hopped on and off the desk in excitement.

Qwilleran phoned her and left his own message: "Come on over anytime. The cats have missed you."

Celia Robinson had rented his carriage-house apartment at one time. She was a fun-loving grandmother who had lived in a Florida retirement complex but decided she preferred snowball fights to shuffleboard. She cooked, did volunteer work, and made everyone happy with her merry laughter.

She happened to be an avid reader of spy and detective fiction, and Qwilleran happened to have an interest in criminal investigation. When suspicions made his moustache bristle, as they often did, he had a compulsion to search for clues, discreetly. What could be more discreet than a secret agent who looked like someone's grandma and laughed a lot? Celia called him "Chief," and he called her "Double-O-Thirteen-and-a-Half."

Then she married the amiable, white-haired Pat O'Dell and moved into his large house on Pleasant Street.

"Faith, an' it's my big kitchen she married me for, I'm thinking," he often said in his rich brogue.

Pat had a janitorial service, and together they started Robin-O'Dell Catering.

Celia interpreted the invitation to "come on over anytime" as "right away" and she arrived in "two shakes of a lamb's tail".

"Do you have time for a glass of fruit juice?" Qwilleran asked, inviting her to sit at the snack bar.

"Oh, you have some new bar stools!" she exclaimed. "Very comfy . . . Where are the kitties?"

"Looking at you from the top of the refrigerator."

Celia groped in her large handbag and they jumped to the floor with two thumps, Yum Yum landing like a feather and Koko landing like a muscular male.

Qwilleran gave them a few crumbles of meat loaf and told them, "This is just the appetizer. The main course will be served at five-thirty."

"Are you enjoying your new career?" he asked her now.

"I love it! But I miss those secret missions, Chief."

"You could still do a little snooping, if you had time, and if Pat wouldn't object."

"He'd never know," she said with a wink. "Do you have any suspicions, Chief?"

"No. Only a nagging curiosity. Who bought the old opera house, and what are they doing with it, and why the secrecy? If I start making inquiries, the gossips will have a field day!"

"I could ask questions. Where would I go?"

"To the courthouse and find out who bought the building. To the City Hall and find out if they've issued any permits for remodeling. It might be a clue to the mystery . . . No hurry, Celia."

"I could do it on Tuesday. Monday we're doing a birthday luncheon in Purple Point. Would anyone mind if Pat and I didn't attend Richard Thackeray's supper? We have to clear away here and go home and get started on the luncheon. How should I explain?"

"There was no RSVP on the invitation," Qwilleran said, "so you don't need to explain. Just do what you have to do. If anyone asks, I'll invent something."

"You're good at that!" she said in admiration. "I think of you every time I buy fruit and vegetables at Toodle's Market." At the recollection she was so overcome with mirth that she choked on her cranberry juice.

"Take it easy!" he said.

In the past, when she uncovered evidence that required the utmost secrecy, there was a clandestine meeting at the market, in the produce department — two casual foodshoppers discussing the price of cucumbers or ripeness of melons, as strangers do. Then she would whisper some amazing revelation too hot to put in writing or entrust to a telephone that might be bugged. The serio-comic charade delighted Celia, who would be forever young. She and Pat still had snowball fights, according to their amused neighbors.

Qwilleran asked her, "How much champagne has been ordered for the reception?"

"Duke has ordered two cases and wants it perfectly chilled, so we're bringing our portable plug-in cooler with temperature control. And the stemware we're renting is glass and not the plastic kind which Duke calls an abomination. He's lending us his grandmother's banquet cloth and ordering a flower arrangement for the table. Since everyone's going to the supper afterward, the cocktail snacks will be bite-size, and Duke wants the very best cheese!!"

When Celia had left, Qwilleran walked down the lane to pick up his daily paper from the newspaper sleeve. He took it to the Art Center porch and sat on the bench there, being impatient to read the Thackeray profile.

There was a three-column photo of Thelma conversing with two parrots and the headline read: THELMA AND FRIENDS COME HOME TO ROOST. Only when she spoke of her five parrots did she wax sentimental. "There were six birds, but Chico passed away. I still have his cage and the cover with his name embroidered on it."

There was plenty of opportunity for name-dropping, and drop them she did. Film celebrities and political figures had come to her dinner club.

She boasted that her twin brother had been a doctor of veterinary medicine. And a boast about her father caused Qwilleran to do a double take. He read it a second time:

"Pop was a hardworking potato farmer, struggling to make a living — until he had a brilliant idea for putting potatoes to a new use. It made him rich! He could send my brother to college and he set me up in business in Hollywood. He invented the low-calorie potato chip!"

At that moment the front door of the Art Center opened, and Thornton Haggis came out, saying, "No loitering permitted!"

"Thorn! Did you see today's paper?" Qwilleran waved the front page at him.

"What happened? Have they found a cure for the common hangover?"

"Sit down and listen!" Qwilleran read the entire profile of the bootlegger's daughter.

"What!" Thornton yelped. "Did she actually say that about potato chips? Does she believe that? Is that what Milo told her? Or did she invent it for Moose County readers?"

"You ask her!" Qwilleran said.

CHAPTER
EIGHT

By Saturday morning Qwilleran had decided that Thelma's potato chip bombshell was a private joke of hers. She had inherited the Moose County penchant for leg-pulling. Only old-timers would appreciate the potato chip quip. That is, old-timers and history buffs.

He phoned Thornton at home to compare theories, and Mrs Haggis answered. "He's out getting his hair cut, Qwill."

"Hair cut!"

"Yes, isn't it a crime? Where has anyone ever seen such a beautiful mop of white hair? But he threatened to dye it green, so I said okay, reluctantly."

"Well, tell him I called. Nothing important."

It was important enough, however, for Qwilleran to call Homer Tibbitt at Ittibittiwassee Estates. He was the only old-timer old enough to remember much about Prohibition.

Rhoda answered in the hushed voice that meant her husband was having one of his many naps.

"Don't disturb him. Did you read about Thelma in yesterday's paper?"

"We did indeed! I read it aloud, and Homer said she was just pulling a fast one . . . Homer says she was a great one for spoofing."

"That's what I wanted to know. When's his birthday?"

"A week from today, and he says he doesn't want any birthday candles or media coverage."

"He's a dreamer, Rhoda. The TV crews will be up here from Down Below to film the event." Qwilleran was careful not to mention that he was writing a birthday song, and arrangements had been made for a serenade by Derek Cuttlebrink with his guitar.

On Sunday morning, a light rain freshened the foliage around Qwilleran's apple barn. In the afternoon a soft sunlight made everything sparkle. By five o'clock the gentlest of gentle breezes was wafting about the bird garden, where the guests were to assemble and Brodie was to pipe a few Scottish tunes.

Qwilleran said, "Whoever is in charge of the local weather decided to show those California dudes a thing or two." He wore his kilt in the red-and-green Mackintosh tartan, together with a green blazer, green knee socks with red flashers, a calfskin sporran, and, of course, a dagger in the sock.

Polly wore a white silk shirtwaist dress with a shoulder sash in the Robertson tartan, that being the Duncan clan connection.

The Siamese had been given an early dinner and dispatched to the gazebo in the canvas tote bag.

The Robin-O'Dell team had set up in the hospitality center with Burgess Campbell's grandmother's Madeira banquet cloth, an arrangement of red carnations and white daisies, an array of sparkling champagne glasses, and trays of tiny canapés, puffs, tartlets, and tasty morsels on toothpicks.

First, Police Chief Brodie arrived, driving up the lane from the back street — the better to get away after piping his stint. He was resplendent in the Brodie clan kilt and shoulder plaid and his bagpiper's feather "bonnet," a good eighteen inches tall.

As the carloads of guests started to arrive, Pat O'Dell was in the barnyard, showing them where to park and steering them to the bird garden. Burgess Campbell and Alexander were in the first carload to arrive — with the Bethunes, his surrogate in-laws. They were all in Highland attire, except the guide dog. There were the MacWhannells and the Camerons, the Ogilvies and MacLeods, all in clan tartans. Mavis Adams and the Morghans, who were not Scots, said they felt like illegal aliens.

The guests strolled around the garden, commented on the plantings, visited the butterfly puddle, and found the gazebo. They looked at the Siamese as if they were creatures in a zoo and the Siamese looked at them in the same way.

Then Pat O'Dell came around the side of the barn and signaled to Qwilleran by jerking his thumb twice over his shoulder, meaning "They're here!" Qwilleran caught Brodie's eye and tapped his wristwatch, and the bagpiper plunged into the attention-getting solemnity of "Scotland the Brave."

What happened in the next few minutes is best described in Qwilleran's own words. He later wrote in his personal journal:

Sunday, April 13 — Standing in the foyer in a formal receiving line was the Royal Family: Queen Thelma, Prince Richard, and the lady-in-waiting. The queen was wearing lavish jewels — and one of her "artistic" hats. Richard lived up to his reputation as a snappy dresser by wearing a Nehru jacket and two-tone shoes.

One by one the guests moved through the line, with introductions made by Fran, who was unusually vivacious. I was the last to be presented to Thelma.

I grasped her hand in both of mine and said warmly, "I've got to talk to you about *that hat*!"

Sounding like Mae West she said, "And I've got to talk to you, Ducky . . . about that . . . *moustache*!" Her facial expression was pleasant, composed, and a trifle arch. "And this is my nephew, Richard Thackeray. Richard, this is the celebrated Mr Q."

He had a good handshake and exuberant personality. "Call me Dick. I know all about you, Mr Q."

"Don't tell anyone," I said.

His voice had a distinct quality — velvety, with an underlying resonance. Later Thelma would tell me that it gave her goose bumps; it was her brother's voice, which four-footed creatures found magnetic, soothing, and even healing.

Janice was the last in the receiving line, her shyness at odds with a kind of eagerness. I couldn't help wondering about her role in the household that had just moved into Pleasant Street.

With the introductions made and everyone holding a glass of champagne, it was time for a toast to the new neighbors. And Burgess did the honors with éclat. Everyone responded noisily and at length. Then Thelma made an acceptance speech, which brought cheers and whistles. I looked at the guide dog to see what he thought of the brouhaha. Alexander, as usual, was completely unflappable.

The group scattered, some clustering around Thelma, others sampling the cocktail snacks or walking up the ramp to be thrilled by the view from the top. Fran escorted Thelma on a tour of the main floor, pointing out decorative features. At one point Fran hissed into my ear, "What's that thing above the fireplace? I told you I could lend you an artwork for the occasion — something more suitable!"

Thelma's chief concern was the lack of television receivers. "Where's your TV?" she demanded, sounding like Bette Davis. "Above the fireplace you could have a fifty-inch screen — the rectangular style for showing movies . . . And with these big, comfortable sofas you'd have a perfect setup for movie parties. I have a large collection of old films that I could lend you."

Dick viewed the recumbent bicycle leaning against a stone wall in the foyer and asked me, "Do you really ride this? How does it feel to pedal with your feet up?"

"When you get used to it, there are many advantages," I told him. "If you'd like to try it, you're welcome to borrow it."

Thelma's assistant was standing alone at the bookshelves that filled much of the wall space on three sides of the fireplace cube. When I approached, she asked, "Have you read all of these?" It was the question I had heard many times from a nonreader.

"Some of them twice, or oftener. If you see a title you'd like to borrow, feel free . . . but if you don't return it, the sheriff will be at your door with a search dog."

The mild jest fell flat. "I don't have time to read books," Janice said. "I read aloud to Thelma — newspapers, that is, and magazine articles . . . Where are the kitties?"

I felt she was changing the subject to avoid personal matters. I may have been wrong. I said, "They're in the gazebo. They don't like large parties. Do you like cats? You might drive Thelma over some afternoon."

"Oh, Thelma doesn't like cats — not at all!" Janice looked about anxiously and said, "Excuse me. I think she wants me."

I felt I was right; Janice was employed to drive the car, cook, and read aloud . . . not to reveal personal details that might reflect on the Thackeray image.

The champagne flowed, guests circulated, and neighbors conversed like long-lost friends.

At one point Polly said to Qwilleran, "I've been listening to talk about the Kit Kat Agenda, and it sounds like a splendid idea! It's the local name for a national movement. Volunteers provide foster homes for unwanted kittens and their mothers, while other volunteers act as adoption agents, matching up the kittens with permanent homes. Burgess, Mavis, and the Bethunes are providing foster care, and Hannah MacLeod is an adoption agent."

Qwilleran said, "But who can tell me about the logistics of foster care?"

"Ask Mavis."

Qwilleran caught up with her at the snack table. "Try one of these delicious cheese puffs," she said.

"I've already had three," he said. "Tell me something about foster care. Where do the temporary cat-families spend their time? Where do they eat and sleep?"

"One needs a spare room for that purpose," Mavis explained. "People go in to talk to them and play with them and introduce them to sociable activity. A kitten that is socialized has more personality and makes a better pet than a poor little thing cooped up in a cage."

"I see the point," he said.

"You should talk to Hannah MacLeod, one of our adoption agents. She's lived here all her life and knows everyone, so she's very successful in finding permanent homes."

Hannah Hawley, a fine contralto, had recently married "Uncle Louie" MacLeod, director of the Mooseland Choral Group, and they were in the process of adopting an eight-year-old boy.

"How's Danny?" Qwilleran asked the couple.

"He's such a bright, personable child," Hannah said. "He loves to go with me when I take prospects to the foster homes to pick out a kitten — or two. Usually two. It's hard to resist a handful of squirming fur looking at you with big eyes and mistaking your finger for something else."

Qwilleran said, "I suppose there's an adoption fee?"

"A modest one, considering that it includes all shots and neutering. To help cover expenses and publicize Kit Kat, we're going to stage a Kit Kat Revue."

Uncle Louie looked at Qwilleran hopefully. "Do you sing or dance?"

"I might be able to write a skit," he replied.

It was nearing seven o'clock, and Qwilleran had talked to everyone but the Bethunes. He found them in the foyer, admiring a long narrow console table. Proudly he told them it was handcrafted, custom ordered by Fran Brodie, and remarkable for the hand-carved dovetailing in the drawers.

"I know," said Doug Bethune. "I'm the one who made the table."

"Shame on you. Why didn't you sign it?" Qwilleran scolded. "A century from now a signed Bethune masterpiece will fetch a couple of million at auction, the way prices are going."

Bonnie said to her husband, "Buy the table back, Doug. Our descendants may need the money to pay the rent!"

"How's Winston?" Qwilleran asked. The Bethunes had adopted the late Eddington Smith's big cat after the bookstore was destroyed.

"He's fine. He hangs out in the library but likes to visit our kitten colony, considering himself a kind of godfather. We have five kittens, but they're all spoken for."

When the guests left for the next festivities — at the Mackintosh Inn — Polly and Qwilleran were the last to leave, and he said to Pat and Celia, who were clearing away the refreshments, "Good show! Let's do it again sometime . . . I've brought the cats in from the gazebo, and Koko is upset about something. Give him some cheese; he'll calm down."

Celia said, "He's mad because he wasn't invited."

Qwilleran thought, He's mad because someone was invited who doesn't have his approval.

Koko was prowling about the barn, sniffing diligently, even snarling and spitting in certain areas for reasons of his own. He was a smart cat, but his actions were not always comprehensible.

Then Qwilleran and Polly drove to the inn.

She said, "The reception was a huge success, and several people commented on the Sibelius numbers, including Thelma. She sounds like Tallulah Bankhead one minute and Katharine Hepburn the next. What do you think about the Kit Kat idea, Qwill?"

"I'm all in favor."

"As Mavis said, it's heartwarming to know that previously unwanted kittens will have a chance to give years of companionship to families and live-alones."

"What did you think about Dick?"

"He's charming! I asked if he thought Thelma would speak to our bird club, and he said she doesn't do formal speeches but he could arrange for a question-and-answer session at the club. He would transport two or three parrots in their cages. He's most cooperative! Thelma's lucky to have him."

Qwilleran huffed into his moustache. "Is he living with them?"

"No. He lives in Lockmaster but has use of the guest room on Pleasant Street."

At the Mackintosh Inn, supper was being served in the ballroom on the lower level. A horseshoe table was set with twenty places and a full complement of candles and flowers. The lights in the chandeliers were turned low. And a trio was playing romantic Hispanic music: accordion, violin, and guitar.

Qwilleran muttered, "They didn't find those guys in Moose County!"

"Probably from Lockmaster," Polly ventured.

There were place cards, and Qwilleran found himself between Thelma and Dick.

Thelma explained, "Perhaps you wondered about "California cuisine." That's what I served in my dinner club — a nouvelle approach, with accents on vegetables and fruits and seafood in dishes created with originality. I always considered James Beard to be my guru. He was from the West Coast, you know. I have twenty-two of his cookbooks."

The music stopped suddenly. Dick said a few words of welcome, and then Thelma surprised everyone by asking a blessing. The music resumed, and servers rolled in carts of lobster and mango in a lemon sauce. This was followed by ramekins of oxtail ravioli, sauced with tomato, basil, and capers. Conversation that was lively at the reception was positively exuberant under the spell of California cuisine.

At one point Dick said to Qwilleran, "What did your barn look like before you bought it?"

"I didn't buy it; I inherited it — a drive-through apple barn with nothing inside but lofts and ladders — plus bats, rats, and wild cats. An architect from Down Below had the vision and determination to make it what it is."

"And a hefty commission, I'll bet. It must have cost you a fortune!"

Qwilleran huffed into his moustache.

Undaunted, Dick went on. "It's a lot of cubic space for one man. If you'd ever feel like recouping your investment, I know a developer who could convert it into an apartment complex."

"A possibility, though not in the foreseeable future," Qwilleran replied stiffly.

Throughout the repast Qwilleran had shown a genuine interest in Thelma's parrots. There were five: Esmeralda, Pedro, Lolita, Carlotta, and Navarro. All were Amazons, noted for their intelligence and conversational ability.

"Come and meet them, Ducky!" was Thelma's enthusiastic invitation. "Come for breakfast tomorrow. Janice will make waffles with fruit sauce. Not too early." A time was set: 10 A.M.

As Qwilleran drove Polly home to Indian Village, he asked, "What did you think of Thelma's hat?" (It had a stiff two-inch brim and puffy crown of layered patches of satin, velvet, damask, and tweed — like leaves, in various shades of green, with a green chiffon sash ending in a handmade green rose.)

Polly said, "Only someone with her good posture and authoritative manner could wear it."

He was on the verge of mentioning his breakfast invitation, but a tremor on his upper lip stopped him. He stroked his moustache with a heavy hand as he returned to the barn from Indian Village.

When Qwilleran arrived home, Yum Yum rubbed against his ankles warmly but Koko was on the fireplace cube, pointedly aloof and obviously disapproving of something. A note from Celia, left on the kitchen counter, explained it:

"Chief — after you left, Koko acted very strange — prowling and bristling his fur and spitting at everything.

I think he smelled the dog. I talked to him and gave him a treat, and he calmed down."

Qwilleran thought, Alexander had been here before, but Koko observed him from the rafters far overhead . . . this time a strange presence was invading his territory in his absence.

He sat down at his typewriter to sum up successes of the evening.

Sunday, April 13 — Well, it's over! Thelma has been adequately welcomed, toasted, and admired — wild hat and all. As usual in such gatherings there is always a gadfly with a tiny camera who flits around taking candid shots of guests eating, yawning, kissing someone else's spouse, or whatever. What do they do with the prints? Are they ever developed? Is there any film in the camera?

Thelma's assistant was the candid-nut tonight, but her shots were all of Thelma. Are the prints catalogued and filed? Or kept in a barrel? They must have thousands of them if . . .

His typing was interrupted by an imperative howl from Koko. The cats' bedtime ritual had been neglected. There was supposed to be a session of reading aloud, followed by a snack and then lights-out.

"Tyrants!" Qwilleran muttered as he followed Koko to the bookshelves. The cat hopped nimbly to an upper shelf and shoved down a leather-bound book. Qwilleran caught it before it reached the floor. (He had been an acclaimed shortstop in college baseball. Who would think that his fielding skill would be put to use in such a mundane manner?) *C'est la vie*, he thought.

Koko's choice was *A Child's Garden of Verses*, and Qwilleran was not in the mood for Robert Louis Stevenson's poetry. "Try again!" he said.

Down came another R.L.S. winner: *The Strange Case of Dr Jekyll and Mr Hyde*. It was vetoed again. "Sorry, but it's not your style."

The three of them finally settled down with the same author's *Travels with a Donkey* until the phone rang.

A woman's hushed and horrified voice said, "Qwill, this is Janice. Don't come tomorrow! Something terrible has happened!"

"Something wrong with Thelma?" he said quickly.

"No. But I can't talk about it. Just don't come tomorrow . . ." and she added in alarm, "Please, don't say anything about this to anyone!"

A few hours after this enigmatic phone call, Qwilleran was asleep in his suite on the first balcony, and the Siamese were supposed to be asleep on the third balcony. He always left their door open (for a number of reasons) and always closed his own. Rudely he was awakened by a bloodcurdling howl outside his door! He knew it well; it was Koko's death howl! The cat had an uncanny way of knowing the moment of a wrongful death. The clock on the night table said it was 3:15 A.M. Immediately it brought to mind the "something terrible" that had happened on Pleasant Street following the party.

But what could he do? Call the police and say that his cat was howling?

Koko had done what he considered his duty and had returned to his balcony. After an hour of puzzling thought and aimless speculation, Qwilleran, too, went to sleep.

CHAPTER
NINE

On Monday morning Qwilleran was listening to the weather prediction on WPKX while preparing the cats' breakfast. It was something choice, left over from the reception, that Celia saved for them. The Siamese watched intently.

Not bothering to turn the radio off, Qwilleran heard newsbites from the two counties to the south. From Lockmaster: A new president had been appointed for the Academy of Arts . . . The date had been set for the annual flower show . . . A local chess player had won a tournament in Milwaukee. From Bixby: A drug bust in Bixton had jailed four men and three women . . . A couple had been killed in a motorcycle accident on Highway 12 . . . An unidentified male was found shot to death at the wheel of a rented van.

At that moment a bloodcurdling howl came from Koko's throat. Once again, it was Koko's death howl. But why was the cat concerned about an unidentified driver of a delivery van in Bixby County . . . unless . . . it had something to do with Janice's cryptic phone call of the night before. There had been horror and fear in her voice. Qwilleran devised an oblique way of investigating.

First, he called Burgess Campbell and congratulated him on a successful party. "Has Pleasant Street recovered from the excitement? Did anyone consume too much champagne or oxtail ravioli?"

"I didn't hear any ambulance sirens," the Duke replied. "And let me say that everyone thanks you for opening your fabulous barn for the occasion."

"My pleasure," Qwilleran said.

"There were some scatterbrained suggestions from the Thackerays," Burgess went on. "Thelma thought the barn would make a wonderful restaurant — with kitchen and bar on the main floor and dining on the open balconies and waiters whizzing up and down the ramp on roller skates . . . And Dick visualized it as a twelve-unit apartment complex, if you wanted to install elevators and a whole lot of plumbing . . . The odd thing is, Qwill, that you can't guess whether they're kidding or being serious."

"Very true, Burgess. I always suspect women who wear crazy hats and men who wear two-tone shoes."

Next, Qwilleran phoned Amanda's Studio of Interior Design and was not surprised to hear that Fran Brodie was taking a week off. He called her in Indian Village.

"Qwill, I'm beat!" she groaned. "No one knows how hard I've worked for that woman — and her inflated ego!"

"You did a heroic job."

"And now she has another design project she wants me to handle. I'm going to sic her on Amanda. That'll be the battle of the century. Thelma Thackeray versus Amanda Goodwinter!"

"What is Thelma's new design project?"

"She's not telling."

"Could it be connected with the old opera house?"

"More likely a restaurant, featuring California cuisine."

"Well, anyway, Fran, you've done admirable work, and I'll make you a marguerita whenever you say."

Qwilleran continued, "That was a lot of partying for a woman of Thelma's age. Have you heard how she is this morning?"

"No, but she was still going strong when I dropped them off at the curb. She invited me in for a nightcap, but I declined and Janice reminded Thelma that she was leaving in the morning for a couple of days in Lockmaster. For someone over eighty, Thelma has a lot of energy. She doesn't drink, she eats right, and she retires at ten P.M. . . . Maybe I should try it!"

The conversation was all very interesting, but it offered no clue to the "terrible" thing that had happened at the Thackeray house. The O'Dells lived across the street, and Pat was known for his powers of observation, while Celia was always a secret agent at heart. But the O'Dells would be on their way to Purple Point with chicken pot pies and blueberry muffins for a birthday luncheon.

Qwilleran left a message on their answering machine under the alias of Ronald Frobnitz. Celia waited until Pat was out of the house before returning the call.

"What's up, Chief?" she asked briskly.

"Did anything unusual happen on Pleasant Street last night?"

"Well, it was quiet and dark until everyone started coming home. Then the street was filled with headlights, and people laughing and shouting goodnight, and kids leaving their pizza party. It had quieted down when Fran Brodie brought the Thackeray party home and dropped them at the curb. Just as they were turning the indoor lights on, I thought I heard a scream. Pat heard it, too, but said it was the parrots. How'm I doin', Chief?"

"If you get tired of the catering business, you can always get a job with the CIA."

"Oh, I remembered something else. Before everyone came home from the party, Pat saw a delivery van drive around the back of the Thackeray house — then leave a few minutes later. We decided it was some kind of fabulous welcome gift that made Thelma scream when she came home."

Qwilleran huffed into his moustache and thought, How does that explain the panic in Janice's voice . . . and the reference to something terrible . . . and the urgent plea not to tell anyone?

"Tomorrow morning, Chief, I'll get that information you want from downtown."

"You can phone it. It's not classified."

"But I want to deliver some chicken pot pies and blueberry muffins, if you think you can use them."

Gravely he said, "I imagine I can devise an appropriate way . . . to dispose of them."

Celia's hoot of delight pierced his eardrum as she hung up.

He had been working on his Tuesday column and now he needed a stretch, so he walked to the public library for the book containing Homer's favorite poem. The parking lot was nearly filled, and the main room was crowded with men and women of all ages. They had seen the announcement in Friday's paper: "Autographed photographs of old movie stars from the Thelma Thackeray collection — on temporary exhibition."

Eight-by-tens in individual easel-back frames filled the shelves in two showcases: Claudette Colbert, Ronald Colman, Groucho Marx, Joan Crawford, Fred Astaire, Humphrey Bogart, Esther Williams, Edward G. Robinson, and more. An occasional comment interrupted the awed silence of the onlookers.

Man: "I'm gonna come back when there ain't such a crowd."

Another man: "Valuable collection! One assumes they're insured."

Woman: "My mother used to rave about Ronald Colman."

Child: "Mommy! Where're the kitties?"

Qwilleran, before leaving the building, stroked the two library cats and dropped coins into the jar that provided for their material needs. "Handsome Mac! Gentle Katie!" he said, wondering if anyone ever read a little Dickens or Hemingway to them.

★ ★ ★

The Siamese were waiting for him with stretched necks and pointed ears: They knew he had been fraternizing with the library cats.

"Read! Read!" he announced, letting them sniff the library book. It was well thumbed, and the binding had been repaired twice by the late Eddington Smith, according to notations inside the back cover. Before taping "Lasca" for Homer's birthday, he would do a practice reading for Koko and Yum Yum.

"Lasca" was written by Frank Desprez. Scene: Texas, down by the Rio Grande. Story: A lonely cowboy hangs around bars, maundering over his lost love, remembering how they rode the range on their gray mustangs. One day, without warning, the weather changed, alarming a herd of steers, goading them into a stampede that trampled everything in its path. When the dust cleared Lasca was dead, but her impulsive act of heroism had saved her lover's life. All was now still on the range, but for a lone coyote, the gray squirrels, a black snake gliding through the grass, a buzzard circling overhead.

Qwilleran paused. It had been more than a hundred lines of galloping rhythm and deep emotion. Yum Yum was breathing hoarsely; Koko uttered a soft yowl.

It was the moment when Rhoda Tibbitt always dried her eyes, and Homer always blew his nose.

The Siamese were sequestered in the gazebo while Qwilleran recorded the poem.

On Tuesday morning Celia marched importantly into the apple barn and reported, "The opera house property has been held by a bank trust for years and years — no new owner . . . and no permits for remodeling have been issued or even requested."

Qwilleran said wryly, "Perhaps the bank is going to rent the space to traveling burlesque shows. The theatre seats were removed long ago, but customers could be told to bring their own floor cushions."

"Oh, Chief!" she protested with her ever-ready laugh. "But I drove by to see what was going on, and there was a van in the parking lot with ladders on top, and it was marked BIXBY PAINT AND DECORATING. Pat says everything is cheaper in Bixby County — goods and services and gasoline. We buy our fresh food at Toodle's Market, but once a week he drives to Bixby to fill up the tank and buy staples."

"Just what I wanted to know, Celia. Have you time for coffee or fruit juice?"

She flopped onto one of the bar stools. "I know you don't go for gossip, Chief, but I've collected some basic intelligence . . ."

"Let's hear it."

"During the party, Thelma's assistant hung around the dining room, and we found we have a lot in common: Both of us have farm backgrounds and both of us are involved in food preparation. Janice is from North Dakota."

"How did she gravitate to Hollywood and the Thackeray household?"

"That's a Cinderella story. She was ten when her mother died, and her father married a woman with three young children. For the next several years, Janice had to help with the kids and the cooking. She had no time for hobbies or sports and felt like dropping out of school and running away from home, but her Aunt Patty made her a deal. If Janice would stay and get her diploma, her aunt would lend her the money to move to a big city and find work in an office. She had taken a commercial course in school.

"Actually she was more interested in cooking than typing and thought Hollywood would have a lot of restaurants as well as glamour.

"Thelma hired her as a dishwasher and Janice worked her way up to assistant chef."

"Did she tell you all this at the party?"

"Well, no . . . She came to the house yesterday morning and asked if she could do anything to help with the luncheon. I took her along in place of Pat; Thelma's out of town. I feel sorry for that young woman. She doesn't have a life of her own. For example, she loves cats but Thelma hates them."

Qwilleran said, "Too bad she didn't get a chance to meet Koko and Yum Yum Sunday night. Would she like to drive over here while her boss is away? She can come anytime but should phone first."

"That's very kind of you, Chief."

He shrugged modestly. Actually, he saw an opportunity to satisfy his curiosity about the canceled breakfast date, but he said, "The cats enjoy meeting a new admirer who will blubber over them. They're only human."

His quips always delighted her, and she asked, "Where are the little dears? I have to say good-bye before I go home." She searched in her big floppy handbag.

"Are you looking for your car keys — or for a possible stowaway, Celia?"

Yum Yum was in the kitchen, batting and chasing a small shiny toy, while Koko peered down from the top of the refrigerator as if amazed by her kittenish antics.

Qwilleran explained, "One of my fans Down Below — an older woman who can no longer see to sew — sent me her sterling silver thimble for the cats to play with. She's the tenth-grade teacher who inspired my writing career. Relatives of hers in Lockmaster send her clippings of my column now and then. I polish the thimble once a week — and hide it in different drawers, but Yum Yum always finds it, and her famous paw can open any drawer that isn't padlocked."

Janice phoned in the late afternoon and arrived soon after in an emerald green coupé.

Qwilleran went out to the barnyard to greet her. "Did you bring this from California?"

"We towed it behind our van full of parrots," she explained.

She was wearing blue denim pants and shirt and wore her dark hair tied back in a ponytail. Other times, it had been knotted close to her head.

He said, "I told the cats you were coming, and they had a good washup. They're waiting for you in the gazebo."

There they were, sitting tall on their haunches, with expectancy in every whisker.

"Aren't they beautiful!" she cried. "Those blue eyes!"

"The one with an imperial air is Kao K'o Kung. Yum Yum likes to be picked up and hugged, but Koko is too macho for lap-sitting."

With his usual perversity, however, Koko was the first to jump on the visitor's lap when she sat down.

"I've never seen Siamese except in pictures," she said. "When I lived on a farm, we had nothing but barn cats."

"That's what these are. Barn cats."

For the first time he heard her laugh. "I wish I'd brought my camera."

"It wouldn't do any good, Janice. They don't cooperate. Koko considers it an invasion of privacy, and naughty Yum Yum poses only for tail shots." This brought another laugh. "Are you interested in photography?"

"Mostly for practical purposes. I've photographed everything in the house for an insurance inventory, and I take a snap of what Thelma wears whenever she appears in public. Just so she won't duplicate, you know."

"Smart idea. May I offer you a glass of white wine? I've chilled a nice white Zinfandel." At the party he had noted that neither she nor Thelma had been drinking champagne, and he had wondered if it might be a Thackeray house rule. Now he would find out.

After a brief pause she said, "Yes, I believe I'd like a glass of wine."

For himself he mixed what was becoming known around the county as the "Q cocktail." Cranberry juice and Squunk water.

There was more conversation about the cats, and Janice hand-fed them a few Kabibbles, saying, "I love the feel of a cat's rough, wet tongue and little, sharp teeth!"

"Do you know about the Kit Kat Agenda?"

"Oh, yes, and I'd love to have kittens . . . but we can't. They have a kitten colony next door, and Duke says I can go over anytime to play with them. It's good for their morale. The housekeeper said the back door is always open; I can just walk in. She's very nice. Everybody's nice around here. They told us it was neighborly to leave the back door unlocked. Thelma thought it was too folksy, but . . . when in Rome, do as the Romans do."

Janice suddenly stopped chattering and looked preoccupied.

Qwilleran said, "Duke lectures on American history at the college, and you might like to audit one of his lectures. They're never dry; he has a sense of humor."

"I'd like that, but it would depend on Thelma's schedule."

"How long have you been with her?"

"Ever since high school. I wanted to work in a restaurant, and she hired me as a dishwasher. That's a general kitchen helper, you know, and I worked my way up to assistant chef at her private dinner club." She was chattering again — nervously, Qwilleran thought. "It was a luxurious club, with a high-ceilinged dining room and crystal chandeliers. Then there was a lounge where you could have cocktails and see old movies on a large screen. In the dining room Thelma moved about the tables, wearing one of her fabulous hats and kidding with the customers, calling them 'Ducky' and swearing in Portuguese, which she learned from the parrots. Everyone loved Thelma and hated to see her retire. She sold the club and kept me on as a secretary, housekeeper, and driver. She's strict — but nice." With a fond smile, Janice added, "She's always quoting things she learned from her pop: *Don't count your chickens before they're hatched . . . Time is money . . . Try to kill two birds with one stone.*"

Qwilleran said, "No wonder she was a success in business . . . May I refresh your drink, Janice?" And casually he added, "It's hard to imagine such a vital personage retiring from the workplace."

"Well, her twin brother died and Dick, her nephew, asked her to come back east."

She paused long enough to make him suspect jealousy between the longtime, hardworking assistant and the charming Johnny-come-lately who was the only living relative. But then she said, "Well, Dick is the kind of person that everyone likes. He cheers her up. But she also treats him like a strict parent." Janice giggled apologetically. "Thelma was born to be boss! Oh, I almost forgot, Thelma would like you to come for waffles Thursday morning at ten o'clock. You can meet the parrots."

Qwilleran jumped up. "I just had a good idea! I happen to have some chicken pot pies and blueberry muffins. We could warm them up and have a picnic supper out there in the gazebo!"

They went indoors, and Janice was privileged to feed the cats while Qwilleran warmed the picnic fare. He also steered the conversation away from the Thackerays.

During the meal he talked about the classes at the Art Center, the clubs that one might join, and the possibilities for volunteer work. "You might like to donate some time to the animal shelter, Janice, and Thelma might find a cause that she could support with her presence."

He felt he was on thin ice, but that's what he wanted.

Janice put down her fork and looked at him with desperate indecision. "There's something I shouldn't talk about . . ."

"Then don't."

"But I want to, and Celia says you're the only one in Moose County that you can trust not to blab . . . Thelma isn't really retired; she's working on a business deal. That's all I can say."

"More power to her!"

"She wanted to go to Lockmaster today to see her brother's grave and the scene of his fatal accident. I don't know why. You'd think it would just upset her."

"It's called closure." He lifted the wine bottle. "Shall I?"

"I'd better not. I'm driving."

"If the worse comes to the worst, I can tow your car home behind my SUV."

The comment brought laughter. She was laughing easily. "Wouldn't Pleasant Street have a picnic with that scene! They don't miss a thing."

Suddenly serious, he said, "That's why your mysterious cancellation Sunday night worried me. You said something terrible had happened, and your neighbors heard screams."

For a moment she was frozen in an attitude of indecision, her eyes darting left and right.

He waited patiently but with encouragement.

"When we got home," she said hesitantly, "the parrots were gone! . . . Kidnapped! And there was a ransom note."

"Did you notify the police?"

"We were afraid to. There were threats — what would happen if we did. So horrible I can't repeat them. Thelma was sick to her stomach."

"Ghastly experience," he said, remembering his gut-wrenching horror when Yum Yum was snatched.

"We had to do what they wanted. Fortunately Dick was there, and he brought them back by daybreak, but he's afraid to talk about it. We've ordered new locks on all the doors and a burglar alarm that rings in the police station . . . For God's sake, don't let Thelma know I told you all this!"

As he accompanied Janice to her car, he asked, "Are you sure you want to drive? I could drive your car and walk home."

"No, no! I'm perfectly all right. Thanks for everything, and we'll see you Thursday morning."

After Janice had driven away, Qwilleran brought the Siamese indoors, and the three of them sprawled in the big chair for a little reading. The cats always enjoyed the sound of his voice and Yum Yum — that little rascal — had discovered the vibration in his rib cage when he was staging a good show.

When Qwilleran closed the book his listeners went on to other activities, and he began to brainstorm:

Who were the kidnappers who made off with five talkative Amazons without detection? No doubt they were readers of the *Moose County Something*. They knew how Thelma treasured her pets. They knew that all of Pleasant Street would be celebrating her arrival at a gala party somewhere else. What was their ransom demand? Large bundles of cash would not be readily available on a Sunday night. Did they want jewels? The parrot pin and matching bracelet had created a stir at the Grist Mill; had Thelma been flaunting her rubies, emeralds, and diamonds at other good restaurants in Moose County and Lockmaster? Whatever the ransom demand, the victims were warned not to notify the police.

And what about Dick? He took a great risk . . . As the saying goes, "Three may keep a secret if two of them are dead." I wouldn't want to be in Dick Thackeray's shoes at this moment!

CHAPTER
TEN

Qwilleran had a strong desire to talk with the photographer who had been assigned to the Thackeray story — called the "parrot story" in the photo lab. John Bushland freelanced for the newspaper but also had his own commercial studio in Pickax, and Qwilleran found him there, early Wednesday morning. Bushy had become a workaholic since his divorce.

"Just wanted to compliment you on the parrot shots, Bushy. What did you think of the old gal?"

"She's a character! You could write a book about her, Qwill."

"I'm invited to meet the parrots tomorrow, and I thought I might pick your brain. How about lunch at Rennie's? I'll buy."

"Well, I've got a lot of printing to do — on deadline. How about picking up some deli sandwiches at Toodle's and bringing them here. I'll make coffee."

Meanwhile, Qwilleran had errands to do. He returned the book of poems to the public library and was on the way out of the building when his curiosity detoured him into the small room devoted to magazines and newspapers. As he hoped, there was a Tuesday copy of the

Bixby Bugle. He remembered the newsbite on WPKX about a murder. No details were supplied except the approximate hour: 3:15 A.M. That happened to be the exact time of Koko's bloodcurdling howl. The headline read: MURDER ON SOUTH SIDE. He scanned it for facts.

Sheriff's deputies, responding to a call early Monday morning, found a van driver slumped over his steering wheel. He had been shot in the head. The victim was carrying falsified ID cards, and the tags on the vehicle were stolen.

The call came in at 3:15 A.M., from the occupant of a mobile home on a country lane south of Bixton.

She said, "My cat woke me up, snarling and growling. The moon was full, and you know how cats are! But there was something else bothering him. Tony is just a plain old tomcat, but he sniffs out trouble like a watchdog."

"So, I looked out the window and saw two vans parked under some trees. They were tail-to-tail, and two men were moving stuff from one van to the other. They were big square boxes, big enough to hold TVs."

"The taillights of the loaded van turned on, and the next thing I knew, I heard a gunshot. I know a gunshot when I hear one. And the loaded van took off in a hurry. That's when I called 911."

Police are investigating. It is thought that the incident is linked with the recent burglary in a television store.

Qwilleran could not help chuckling. He was no admirer of the reporting in the *Bixby Bugle*, but here was a dry piece of police news that had been turned into a human-interest story, complete with a hero-cat who sniffed out foul play. Tony would make a good partner for Koko. If they could locate a third talented feline in Lockmaster, they would have a tri-county crime-detection network.

Such were his whimsical thoughts at the moment, but he had sandwiches to buy and other matters to discuss at the photo studio, and a tape to deliver.

The question occurred to him: How could Koko know — and why would he care — about the murder of a shady character ninety miles away? There were no answers; Qwilleran had stopped trying to find answers.

Next he drove to Ittibittiwassee Estates, the retirement complex masquerading as a Swiss resort hotel. Using the house phone, he called upstairs and said in a brisk voice, "Mrs Tibbitt, there is a gentleman here who says he has a package for you and wants to hand it to you personally. He has a large moustache and looks suspect. Do you want us to call the police? It could be a bomb."

With her hand muffling her hysterical laughter, she said, "I'll be right down. Tell him not to go away."

Soon, a white-haired woman, looking gaily youthful, stepped off the elevator. After all, Rhoda was only eighty-eight; her husband would be ninety-nine on Saturday.

"Thank you so much, Qwill. What did you think of the poem?"

"Recording it was an enjoyable challenge, and the cats liked it, especially the stampede and the part about the coyote and the black snake. What is the program for Saturday?"

"At eleven A.M. Derek will sing a birthday song written expressly for Homer — that boy is so talented! — and there'll be city and county dignitaries and media coverage. No birthday cake! Homer says he doesn't want to squander his last breath on blowing out candles."

"By the way, Rhoda, you used to teach in Lockmaster, didn't you?"

"Yes. That's where I met Homer. He was principal of my school."

"Did you know of a Dr Thackeray, veterinarian?"

"Oh, yes! He was a wonderful man — used to come to the school and talk to the younger grades about the proper care of pets. He was killed in a tragic accident. He loved the outdoors and was hiking when he slipped on wet rocks and fell into a ravine."

Qwilleran stroked his moustache repeatedly when he thought of Dr Thackeray; he wanted to ask more questions. He stopped at the design studio, knowing that Fran's assistant would be minding the shop.

Lucinda Holmes greeted him, brimming with her usual hospitality, but before she could suggest coffee, he said, "No coffee today, thanks. Just answer a question. Do you take your animals to the Thackeray Clinic?"

"It's the Whinny Hills Clinic now. Some new people bought it after Dr Thurston's tragic death. That's where my boyfriend works."

"You mean . . . Dr Watson?"

"You remembered!" she said with an appreciative laugh. In a lowered voice she added, "He's not too happy. His new bosses promised to maintain Dr Thurston's standards, and they even have his photo in the lobby, but it's only to please his former clients — and his son."

"Do you know Dick Thackeray?"

"I met him once at a party. All I remember is his wonderful smile. But they say he cracked up after his father's death and had to go away for a while. It was thought to be suicide, you know, and that must have been especially painful."

"Was the doctor hiking alone?"

"Yes, and when he didn't return, his son notified the police. It took the rescue squad seven hours to find him. Very sad. So I don't know . . ."

"Too bad," Qwilleran murmured.

John Bushland liked the nickname of "Bushy"; it made his baldness a joke instead of a calamity. He and Qwilleran had been friends ever since being shipwrecked on a deserted island — only a dozen miles offshore from Mooseville but cold and wet and unforgettable.

On this occasion they got together over corned-beef sandwiches and cream of asparagus soup. "I've just heard, Bushy, that your portrait of Thurston Thackeray hangs in the lobby of the Whinny Hills Clinic."

"Yeah, he sat for a formal portrait when I had my photo studio in Lockmaster. He was a good subject — patient, composed, cooperative."

"Do you visualize him as a suicide?"

"Nah! I never bought that rumor. Somebody was trying to make a scandal out of a sad mishap. People can be rotten."

"Well, the reason I called," Qwilleran said, "is because Thelma has invited me over to see her parrots tomorrow. What's your take on that?"

"I dunno. She's hard to figure. Secretive, and yet avid for publicity. Mad about her parrots but turned-off about any other animals . . . I liked her assistant, Janice — very helpful and down-to-earth."

"Did you meet Thelma's nephew?"

"Nope. That would be Doc Thurston's son."

"What's his line of work?"

"Financial management, whatever that means. Investments, I suppose. When I lived in Lockmaster, the joke was that Dick had inherited his father's love of horses, and that's why he spent so much time at the racetrack."

"Have you put your boat in the water as yet?"

"Last weekend. Would you like to go for a cruise to Three Tree Island?" It was said slyly.

"Bad joke," Qwilleran muttered. "I'd rather cut my wrists."

"I'm taking Jill Handley and her husband for a cruise Sunday. She met Janice when we were doing the parrot story and suggested it would be friendly to invite her out on the boat. Janice is new in town and doesn't know anybody."

"I'm sure Janice would like it," Qwilleran said, "but she doesn't have any regular days off . . . However . . . I might be able to pull strings. I'll phone you tomorrow afternoon."

On the way home from lunch Qwilleran suddenly realized that he had done nothing about Friday's column, nor did he have the ghost of an idea. He had allowed his work-pattern to be disrupted by a kidnapping, an unexplained death, work on an abandoned building, and an elderly woman's idiosyncrasies.

On such occasions he had a game he played with Koko. The cat liked to push books off the shelf, then peer over the edge to see how they landed. Qwilleran, having failed to discourage the practice, devised a way to put it to good use. He would give the signal, and Koko would dislodge a book. Then Qwilleran was required by the rules to base a "Qwill Pen" column on that title. There was something about the imperative of the game that stimulated creative juices. It sounded silly, but it worked.

Now, Koko was on the shelf, peering over the edge with satisfaction at a slender book in a worn cover, one of the last to come from the used-book store in its final days. Qwilleran took the book, along with the cats and the cordless phone, to the gazebo. It was a book of proverbs, and he was fingering it and searching for inspiration when the phone rang.

Fran Brodie was calling to say, "I'd like to collect that marguerita you promised me."

"When!" Qwilleran asked sharply.

"Now!" she replied crisply.

"Where are you?"

"In your backyard."

When he went to the barnyard to meet her, she added apologetically, "I hope I'm not interrupting your work."

"That's all right. I'm sure you won't stay long."

"Touché!"

"Come indoors."

She perched on a bar stool while he prepared her favorite cocktail. "I'm here," she said, "because I heard you're going to visit the parrots tomorrow."

"Do you think I should have a psittacosis shot? Who told you?"

"Dwight." She referred to their mutual friend, who was handling public relations for Thelma. "If you're planning to do a Thackeray story, Dwight thinks you should avoid mentioning the interior design. And so do I!"

It was an unusual request from the designer who had just received an enormous commission.

They took their drinks into the living room, where Fran saw the wall hanging over the fireplace. "I see it's still there," she said with a sniff.

He ignored the remark. "So, what's the problem at Thelma's house? I'm invited for a waffle breakfast and a social call on Pedro, Lolita, and company. If I write anything, it'll be a legend for *Short & Tall Tales*. What are you trying to tell me about the decorating — excuse me. The interior design."

"Have you been in any other houses on Pleasant Street?"

"Two or three."

"Then you know they all have wallpaper, stained woodwork, draperies, and Oriental rugs on hardwood floors. Thelma shocked us by wanting stark white walls, white-painted woodwork, white mini-blinds, and — worst of all! — wall-to-wall white vinyl cemented to the beautiful oak floors. What could we do? It's her house! Amanda believes in letting the customers have what they want. Her modern furniture looks perfect with that background . . . but not on Pleasant Street!"

"Sticky wicket!" Qwilleran said.

"I know you like contemporary, Qwill, in all its forms, so you'll probably like it. But both Dwight and I feel that it would not be to anyone's advantage to have the interior published. So concentrate on the parrots, her collection of designer hats, her waffles, and her infatuation with old movies."

"Hmmm," he mused as he picked up her empty glass. "Shall I try it again? Maybe I'll get it right."

She jumped to her feet. "No, thanks. We're having a family get-together tonight. I have to be there — and sober."

As Qwilleran watched her drive away, he speculated that there was no family get-together. Fran wanted to avoid answering questions about Thelma's secret business enterprise. He was certain now that it involved the old opera house. Earlier in the day he had driven past the site and stopped to watch moving vans unloading large cardboard cartons. Each had the manufacturer's name and large letters spelling out ONE CHAIR or ONE TABLE.

★　★　★

Qwilleran went directly to the phone and called Dwight Somers.

He was still in his office. "Qwill! It's been a long time! Are you staying out of trouble?"

"Yes and it's boring. Are you free for dinner? We could go to Onoosh's and plot something illegal."

Dwight Somers had the kind of face that looks better with a beard — stronger, wiser. He had come to Moose County from Down Below — to handle public relations for XYZ Enterprises. Disagreeing with the management over the development of an offshore island, Dwight resigned and joined a P.R. agency in Lockmaster. Their company policy was: no beards. Too bad. Devoid of whiskers he looked clean-cut, honest, and younger, but not strong or wise. He eventually left to start his own P.R. firm in Pickax. He called it Somers & Beard, Incorporated.

"Now you look like Dwight Somers!" Qwilleran told him when they met at the Mediterranean café. They sat in a booth for privacy. There were beaded curtains in the windows, hammered brass tops on the tables, and spanakopita on the menu.

Politely, Qwilleran asked about Indian Village (where Dwight had an apartment) and about Hixie Rice (with whom he was seen everywhere).

Dwight asked politely about the Siamese.

"I hear you're handling public relations for Thelma Thackeray. How is she to work with?"

"I talk to her like a big brother. I tell her that people have a tendency to be critical, jealous, and antagonistic when a local son or daughter returns with money, fame, and glamour. My job is to let these people know what a friendly, generous person she is. We've lined up donations to all local charities and fifteen churches — the latter in memory of her dear "Pop." She's no public speaker, but she'll appear at social events and answer questions about parrots, old movies, and hats as an art form."

"I understand," Qwilleran said, "that you want me to avoid mention of the interior design." As a journalist he should resent being told by a P.R. man what to write . . . but this was a small town, and there was more than Thelma's public image to be considered.

"Fran and I have discussed it. Stark white décor is high style in some parts of the U.S. and abroad, but the concept is far-out for Moose County. Nothing would be gained by shocking the gossips and turning off the general public. Meanwhile we can accentuate the positive by concentrating on the parrots."

Qwilleran said, "And waffles, and art hats, and old movies. I'm no expert on interior design, anyway, although I know what I like, and I like most contemporary stuff. You could help me, Dwight, by telling me about her new business venture, which seems to be a deep dark secret. Has she bought the old opera house?"

"It's been in her family for seventy-five years. It's been rented for everything from government purposes in wartime to appliance storage in peacetime."

"Is she opening a restaurant? I've seen tables and chairs being delivered."

Dwight lowered his voice. "It's to be a film club, cabaret style . . . with the latest and best in projection equipment and sound system and screen . . . for viewing old movies exclusively."

After dinner, Qwilleran shut himself up in his office on the balcony and went to work on the Friday column. The question was: How to make it interesting to the readers? The answer was: Make them think. Keep them guessing . . . Give them something to talk about. He wrote:

WHO SAID THIS?

Three may keep a secret if two of them are dead. You have three guesses. Here are some clues:

He was a philosopher, publisher, scientist, diplomat, mathematician, postmaster general, signer of the Declaration of Independence, vegetarian, and genius. He invented the idea of daylight saving time long before it was adopted. And he invented the incredible glass harmonica. In case you have not yet guessed . . . you'll find his portrait on the hundred-dollar bill.

This Renaissance Man of eighteenth-century America also found time to write collections of wit and wisdom and publish them over a period of twenty-five years under the pen name of Richard Sanders. (They became known as *Poor Richard's Almanac.*) Included are sayings that everyone knows, like *Make haste slowly* and *Time is money*. Some have a trace of cynicism: *Where there is marriage without love, there will be love without marriage.*

Qwilleran ended his column with a quiz, challenging his readers to test their worldly wisdom. He informed them that the answers would be in his "Qwill Pen" column on Tuesday.

Pleased with his work, he had a large dish of ice cream, then walked three times around the barn with a flashlight, thinking . . .

The next day would start with waffles at Number Five Pleasant Street and a get-acquainted session with the parrots. Would they be nervous after being snatched by strangers in the middle of the night? How much would Thelma want to say about her Lockmaster trip? Did Dick take her to dinner at the five-star Palomino Paddock? Who picked up the check?

He could think of many questions to ask, but they were all out-of-bounds: Do you think the kidnappers followed you from California? If not, did they learn about the much-loved parrots from Friday's newspaper? Did the interview reveal that all the neighbors would be away, feting the newcomer? What was the ransom demand? How could anyone scrape up a large amount of cash on a Sunday night? Do kidnappers now accept checks or credit cards? (Bad joke.) So was it Thelma's jewels they wanted? How did they know she had ten-thousand-dollar lapel pins and fifteen-thousand-dollar bracelets?

CHAPTER
ELEVEN

On the night before the waffle breakfast Qwilleran tuned in the WPKX weathercast, knowing he would hear nonsense as well as reasonably accurate predictions. His friend Wetherby Goode was more entertainer than meteorologist, but that was what the good folk of Moose County wanted. He always had a few lines of poetry, song, or nursery rhyme to fit the weather.

At least once a week he dedicated a forecast to someone in the news, such as Lenny Inchpot when he won the bicycle road race and Amanda Goodwinter when she was elected mayor.

On Thursday he dedicated his predictions to "Thelma Thackeray, who grew up here and has returned to God's country after a long career someplace in California . . . Thelma, you may have forgotten that we have interesting weather here. This morning is sunny with temperatures in the upper seventies, but if you go out, take a jacket and umbrella, because there will be light rain and a chill breeze — that is, if you don't want to catch cold. But if you do get the sniffles, drink some hot lemonade and put a goose-grease plaster on your chest."

Then he sang a few lines about "raindrops falling on my head" accompanying himself on the studio piano.

If Thelma happened to be listening, she would scream with laughter at the mention of goose-grease. Old-timers in Moose County, reminiscing about the "bad old days," always guffawed over the hot, scratching, smelly horrors of a goose-grease plaster.

To Qwilleran's recollection he had eaten waffles only once in his life, and it behooved him to educate himself. A phone call to the public library launched a volunteer on a spirited search.

Thanks to her efforts, he learned that waffles have been around since Ancient Greece . . . that the first waffle iron in the United States was patented in 1890 . . . that waffle irons were the most popular wedding gift in the first quarter of the twentieth century . . . that there was at least one waffle iron in every respectable attic in Moose County.

As the time came to leave for breakfast, the cats watched him with anxious blue eyes, as if they expected never to see him again. "Would you like to send your regards to Pedro and Lolita?" he asked.

Pleasant Street was quiet — ten gargantuan wedding cakes waiting for a wedding. The most flamboyant was Number Five. The front door, called the carriage entrance, was on the side, and Janice was waiting for him in her cook's apron and floppy hat.

"Good morning," she said. "Isn't it a lovely day?"

He handed her the bunch of carnations in green tissue that he had picked up on the way over. His instinct had told him to choose brilliant red.

"Thelma will love them!" Janice said. "She's running a little late. Shall I bring you coffee while you're waiting?"

The wait gave him a chance to appraise the decorating. He thought it had elegance and joie de vivre. The whiteness of it all reminded him of a white-on-white artwork he had won in a raffle at the Art Center. Against the totally white background, however, exciting things were happening: A sofa and chairs with ebony frames in contemporary mission style had square-cut seats and back cushions in steel gray silk. Cool! he thought. They were accented with puffy down-filled toss pillows in parrot colors: vivid green, brilliant red, and chrome yellow. Tables were stainless steel with plate-glass tops. Handmade art rugs, large and small, defined the areas. Wall art consisted of large contemporary paintings and tapestries that stayed on the wall instead of jumping out at the viewer.

He was attracted to a pair of tall, narrow étagères in the foyer — stainless-steel frames, each with five plate-glass shelves graduated in width. The frames flared upward, so that the shelf space at the top was wider than the shelf space at the bottom. It was a concept that gave grace and lightness to the design. The Moose County approach, Qwilleran thought, would be: straight-up-and-down like a ladder.

The shelves were filled with an astounding collection of tropical birds in brilliantly glazed porcelain. As

116

Qwilleran examined them, he became aware of a strong presence: Thelma was descending the stairs with one braceleted hand grasping the handrail and the other braceleted hand extended in welcome. She was wearing a simple caftan in brilliant yellow that accentuated the silvery gray of her hair — a short-crop with bangs.

Qwilleran said, "Your home, Thelma, has an air of elegance plus a certain joie de vivre!"

"Bless you, Ducky! You talk just like you write! And you look even handsomer than you did at the party! . . . Follow me! Waffles will be served in the breakfast room. I hope you like them as much as we do!"

In the breakfast room Qwilleran was served crisp, buttery waffles flavored with toasted pecans and topped with an apple-date sauce. He declared they were the best he had ever tasted in his life. (His previous experience had been in a fast-food place in New Jersey.) "What do the parrots have for breakfast?" he asked, to nudge the conversation in another direction.

"Standard parrot feed," Thelma said, "plus treats like safflowers seeds, apples, bananas, celery, and raw peanuts. They love chocolates and marshmallows, but we don't want them to get fat."

Janice said, "Dick gave Lolita a chocolate-covered caramel, and her beak got all gummed up. It was funny to watch her struggle, but she liked it and wanted more."

"I don't approve of Dick's cute tricks, and I've told him so!" his aunt said sternly.

Twice, in asides to each other, the two women had referred to a "Mr Simmons."

"Who is Mr Simmons?" Qwilleran asked. "Your probation officer?"

Janice squealed in glee; Thelma murmured her amusement and said, "He's a retired police detective who worked for me at the dinner club. He was a security guard in dinner jacket and black tie, and he felt it his responsibility to protect my personal safety."

"He had a crush on Thelma," Janice said mischievously.

"When I sold the club and retired, he became a friend of the family, coming to dinner once a week and keeping an eye on everything. He adored Janice's cooking. When he learned we were moving east, he insisted on giving me a small handgun and showing me how to use it, being concerned about two women crossing the continent alone. He is a dear, sweet man."

Qwilleran said, "I hope no one ever calls me a dear, sweet man."

"Don't worry, Ducky; they won't," Thelma retorted.

That was what he liked about her — her edge.

Qwilleran had avoided asking obvious questions about the parrots, since the answers had been in Friday's feature story, which he should have read. Actually he had given it a quick scan, so he played it safe. "How was your sight-seeing in Lockmaster, Thelma?"

"The horse country is pretty . . . and the restaurants are quite good . . . though not as good as mine, Ducky!" she said with a confidential wink. Then she said soberly, "What I really went to see was my brother's grave. I told Dick to leave me alone for a few

118

minutes and I visited with dear Bud . . . and said a little prayer . . . Then I wanted to see the gorge where he and Sally used to hike, and where he had his accident. Dick stayed at the car — he said it was too gruesome. But I thought it was beautiful. There was a trestle bridge in the distance that looked as if it was made of toothpicks, and while I watched, a little toy train roared across it. There was a river far down below."

"The Black Creek," Qwilleran said.

"When Pop used to bring us to Lockmaster for a picture show, we never saw anything like the gorge. He'd hitch up the wagon, and my stepmom would make pasties, and we'd have a picnic lunch. Tickets to the picture show were a nickel, so that was twenty cents for four. Pop didn't often splurge."

"Do you remember the first movie you ever saw?"

"How could I forget? It was *Ben Hur* with all those chariot races! Silent, of course . . . then *The Circus* with Charlie Chaplin. How we loved the little tramp! . . . The first picture with sound was *The Jazz Singer* and that's when I decided I wanted to be *in pictures*, as they said then. By that time we weren't so poor and could go oftener."

Qwilleran asked, "When did movies come to Pickax?"

"Bud and I turned twelve, and Pop gave us the Pickax Movie Palace for a birthday present. It had been the old opera house — closed for ages — and he said he got it cheap. That's when we started seeing Garbo, John Barrymore, Gable, and the Marx Brothers. We saw *Duck Soup* three times. When I saw *The Gay Divorcee* with Ginger Rogers and Fred Astaire, that's when I knew I had to go to Hollywood."

Janice had the waffle iron at the table, and Qwilleran was indulging himself.

"Shall we take our coffee into the aviary?" Thelma suggested.

All the houses on Pleasant Street had been designed with a front parlor and a back parlor, the latter being the family room in contemporary parlance. At Number Five it was called the aviary, however. Half of the space was behind chain-link fencing reaching to the ceiling. The other half was comfortably furnished with wicker tables and chairs and indoor trees in brass-bound tubs.

Inside the giant cage all was aflutter with color and life as parrots teetered on perches, showed off on trapezes, or climbed the chain-link, using their feet and strong beaks. One powerful beak was chewing on a tree branch. At the same time there was chattering, whooping, conversing in two languages, and noisy flapping of wings.

In the background were six single-occupancy cages, five of them with doors open and night-covers rolled back. A cover with the embroidered name CHICO stood alone.

"Who's Chico?" Qwilleran asked. "Is he in the dog-house?"

"Our dear Chico died three years ago," Thelma said. "We keep his cage as a memorial to a very remarkable bird."

Qwilleran said, "I must say they're an engaging crew!" He could imagine how tormented Thelma must have been when they were stolen.

They sat in the wicker chairs with their coffee, and Qwilleran said, "In Friday's paper you were quoted as saying that Amazons are unusually intelligent and talkative, and that yours hold conversations in English and Portuguese. How do birds, no matter how intelligent, learn human speech?"

"They mimic the people they live with, including babies, cats, dogs, and voices on television," Thelma said. "Pedro used to live with a professor in Ohio and has a working vocabulary of two hundred words. He also likes to talk politics. That's Pedro, chewing on a tree branch."

"Powerful beak," Qwilleran said. "I wouldn't want to meet him in a dark alley."

"He's called a Blue Front. Others are: Yellow Nape and Red Lore — all are wonderfully colorful when they fan their tails and fluff their nape feathers."

Qwilleran said, "The one with a white circle around the eye seems especially alert and listening to everything we say."

"That's Esmeralda. She lived with a musical family and has a large repertory of patriotic songs, popular tunes, and operatic arias. Unfortunately she doesn't know anything all the way through. Carlotta can recite the Greek alphabet but only as far as kappa . . . Navarro does a perfect wolf-whistle . . . They pick up whatever they hear . . . The two sitting with beaks together like a couple of gossips are Lolita and

Carlotta. They keep looking at your moustache, Qwill — trying to figure out how to steal it. Amazons are very mischievous, you know."

Qwilleran stood up. "The situation is getting dangerous! In the interests of sartorial safety, I must leave."

She responded with her soft little laugh — a musical "hmmm hmmm hmmm."

Then soberly he said as they walked to the door, "Have you ever seen the grave of your father, Thelma?"

"I don't even know its location!"

"I do. It's a beautiful site. I'd like to drive you there Sunday afternoon. And we could have dinner at the Boulder House Inn overlooking the lake."

"Bless you!" she cried.

As he was leaving, he asked casually, "Okay to write a "Qwill Pen" column on the Amazons? If so, I'll have to come back and take notes."

He was aware of Janice's petrified stare, but he concentrated on Thelma's reaction. She caught her breath and paused slightly before saying, with equal nonchalance, "The cocky little devils have had all the publicity they deserve. Thanks, but no thanks."

"Too bad," Qwilleran said, "I was looking forward to having some dialogue with Pedro on politics."

"Yes, he has some opinions," Thelma said, "but they're not always printable."

On the way home he pulled off the road and phoned Bushy, leaving a message on his answering device: "Go ahead and invite Janice for a boat ride. I'm taking Thelma sightseeing Sunday afternoon."

It was not long before Thelma called the barn:

"Qwill, that photographer who took pictures of the parrots has invited Janice for a boat ride Sunday, with a picnic lunch on an island. The reporter who was here and her husband are invited, too. I'd like Janice to meet some people of her own age, but I'm wondering if it's entirely — safe."

Was she worried about a seaworthy craft? A competent pilot? Decent weather? Or what?

He said, "John Bushland comes from a long line of lake navigators and grew up at the pilot wheel. And Jill Handley's husband owns the health food store downtown, so you know the lunch will be safe, too."

That evening, when Qwilleran and Polly had their usual phone-chat, he said, "Would you mind if I took another woman to dinner on Sunday?" He waited for her to splutter a question and then explained. "Thelma has never seen her father's grave at Hilltop Cemetery and I thought it would be a kind gesture if I took her there and then to the Boulder House for Sunday dinner."

"Why Boulder House?" she asked more or less curtly.

"It's picturesque and historic." Actually, he saw it as a chance to tease the potato chip heiress.

Toward the end of the evening, when it was still too early for lights-out, he sprawled in his lounge chair with his feet on the ottoman and thought about the next "Qwill Pen" column — and the next — and the next. A columnist's job, he liked to say, is 95 percent "think" and 5 percent "ink." Koko was staring at him. One could never tell whether he was beaming a message about food or a lofty idea for the "Qwill Pen." Qwilleran agreed with Christopher Smart, the poet who maintained that staring at one's cat will fertilize the mind.

What transpired on this occasion may have been the cat's idea or his own; no one was keeping score. The fact was that Qwilleran's mind drifted to Tony, the Bixby tom-cat . . . and the two vans . . . and the large boxes thought to contain stolen TV sets . . . Could they have been parrot cages, shrouded with custom-tailored night covers? If so, the person who drove away from the scene fast could have been Dick, the hero of the abduction incident. In that case, it was Dick who killed the kidnapper. And if so, did he recover the ransom from the dead man's possession?

But then he thought: The rescuer of the parrots could have been a go-between, an unscrupulous lout, paid for his services. That being the case, did the go-between pocket the ransom after delivering the birds and killing the poor clod behind the steering wheel? How many of the devils collaborated on the plot?

And then he thought: Was Dick one of the collaborators?

The idea was abhorrent, although — as Shakespeare observed — one can smile and smile and be a villain.

"Yow!" was Koko's strident announcement. After all, it was five minutes after the time for their bedtime snack.

The days that followed were unusually busy for Qwilleran, and there was no time for frivolous conjectures about the kidnapping. Indeed, he had to admit that the large, square objects mentioned in the *Bixby Bugle* might have been stolen television sets, as the police said.

CHAPTER
TWELVE

When Qwilleran handed in his copy for Friday's paper, Junior scanned it and said, "We'd better alert the bank to get some hundred-dollar bills out of the vault. People around here think that nothing over a twenty is negotiable."

Qwilleran commented, "That was a nice piece on the Kit Kat Agenda in yesterday's paper."

"Yeah, Mavis Adams makes a good interview. She has all the facts, and she's articulate. She's an attorney, you know, although she doesn't look like one."

"What is a woman attorney supposed to look like, Junior? After all, you don't look like a managing editor."

Ignoring the barb, Junior said, "Wait till you see the big ad on page five —"

He was interrupted by the breezy arrival of Hixie Rice. "Hi, you guys! What's new and exciting?"

"Old proverbs," Qwilleran replied. "Just to test your cultural literacy, see if you can finish this one. *Three comforts of old age are . . .*"

Neither she nor the managing editor could fill in the blanks.

"I'm ending my column with a quiz. Readers will be given the three or four opening words of several proverbs. If they can't complete them, the answers will be in my Tuesday column."

"So what are the three comforts of old age?" they wanted to know.

"You'll have to wait until Tuesday."

Hixie objected. "That's too long a wait. Readers will lose interest. I have a better idea. Bury the answers in today's paper — in the want ads, real estate listings, or wherever."

Junior, always under Hixie's spell, seconded the motion, and Qwilleran was outvoted. Reluctantly he handed over the answers, and Junior rushed them off to the production department.

Qwilleran asked Hixie, "And how are the plans progressing for the Sesquicentennial?"

With her usual enthusiasm she said, "The committee has tons of ideas! And we have a whole year to work on it! It's going to be the biggest little Sesquicentennial in North America!"

"More power to you!" he said.

Qwilleran's next chore was to take Polly's long shopping list to Toodle's Market, and in the paper goods aisle his loaded cart collided with that of a Pleasant Street resident. "Sorry," he said. "I have insurance, in case I've broken your eggs, or curdled your coffee cream."

It was Jeffa, the new wife of Whannell MacWhannell. "Qwill! Isn't that a large load of groceries for a bachelor and two cats?"

"They're Polly's," he explained. "I do her shopping while she's at work, and then I get invited to dinner."

"Smooth! I never had an arrangement like that when I was in the workplace . . . By the way, that was an excellent feature on the Kit Kat Agenda in your paper."

"Are you involved?"

"Mac has okayed a kitten colony as long as they have their own room and don't run all over the house getting in his shoes and pants legs. There's a meeting Tuesday night to plan the Kit Kat Revue. I hope you'll be there."

When Qwilleran returned to the barn, Yum Yum greeted him with affectionate ankle-rubbing, but Koko was sitting stiffly and defiantly on one of the bookshelves.

Qwilleran thought, That rascal! He's knocked it down again, just to be funny.

The book on the floor was not *Poor Richard's Almanac* but another old book from the late Eddington Smith's store: a historical novel by Winston Churchill. And that raised a question:

Eddington had named his cat Winston Churchill — a dignified gray longhair with plumed tail and an impressive intellect. The bookseller attributed the latter to the cat's literary environment. Now it occurred to Qwilleran that Winston had been named for an American author — not a British statesman! The book on the floor was a historical novel about the American Revolution published in the late nineteenth century.

Titled *Richard Carvel*, it was by the most popular author of historical novels of his time.

At two o'clock, Qwilleran walked down the lane to pick up his newspaper. Eager to read the ad on page five, he sat on the bench at the front door of the Art Center.

The ad announced the opening of Thelma's Film Club in the old opera house featuring old movies from the Golden Age of Hollywood . . . for members only . . . cabaret style. Beer and wine at the evening show and a full bar at the late-night show. There was a phone number to call for further information. It was a Lockmaster exchange.

As Qwilleran was marshaling the questions he wanted to ask, the front door of the Art Center was flung open, and Thornton Haggis shouted, "Hey, Qwill! What kind of tricks are you playing on your long-suffering readers?" He was waving a copy of the *Something*. "I've been through this whole paper, line by line, and I can't find a single reference for your readers about old sayings!"

"Oh-oh! Let me use your phone," Qwilleran said.

In the office he got Junior on the phone. "What happened!"

The managing editor groaned. "It was all set up for the business page! And it disappeared! Don't ask me how. Our phone has been ringing nonstop. Hixie's doing a recorded message: *If you wish the answers to the 'Qwill Pen' quiz, please press one.* Then the nine sayings are read . . . There's always something, isn't there, Qwill?"

Another of Hixie's ideas had gone awry. Qwilleran began to fear for the Sesquicentennial.

When he arrived at the barn, Qwilleran phoned the *Moose County Something* and "pressed one" as instructed. A voice said, "We apologize for the computer error that omitted the answers to the proverb quiz in the "Qwill Pen" column. The correct answers are . . ."

1. Three comforts of old age are an old wife, an old dog, and ready money.
2. A cat in gloves catches no mice.
3. An empty bag can never stand upright.
4. Eat to live and not live to eat.
5. A used key is always bright.
6. He that lives on hope dies of starvation.
7. There never was a good war or a bad peace.
8. Blame-all and praise-all are two blockheads.
9. Keep your eyes wide open before marriage and half shut afterward.

When Qwilleran arrived at Polly's condo for dinner, he used his own key to let himself in and was met by Brutus with a challenging stare.

He said to the cat, "Do you want to see my driver's license or social security card? Or will my press card do?"

"Come in! Come in!" Polly called from the kitchen, "and tell me what went wrong at the *Something* today? The library was swamped with calls!"

"What did they want?"

"The answers to your quiz — that should have been in the paper and weren't. We looked up the sayings in *Bartlett*, and the clerks have been reading them off to callers."

He said, "You always have everything under control, Polly. Shall we have dinner on the deck? The temperature is perfect; there's no wind."

"Any bugs?"

"Too early."

The first course was a grapefruit compote with blueberries and he said, "I don't remember any grapefruit on your shopping list today."

"Wait till you hear the story! ... One of our volunteers received a shipment of grapefruit from an orchard in Florida — with birthday greetings from someone called Miranda. She doesn't know anyone by that name, and her birthday is in November. She phoned the orchard. They didn't seem concerned — just blamed computer error and told her to enjoy them ... Well, she's a widow, living alone, so she brought them to the library."

"It seems to me," Qwilleran said, "that the computers make more errors than humans ever did."

"And human errors seemed more understandable and forgivable."

"I must say it's the best grapefruit I ever tasted. Welcome to the Brave New World of Computer Errors."

The main course was a casserole combining several recent leftovers, and Qwilleran congratulated her on creating a flavor hitherto unknown to the human palate, even though it looked like a dog dinner. "It beggars description," he said. "I hope there are seconds." They consumed it in a silence of rapture or stoicism.

"And now are you ready for the salad, dear?"

"As ready as I'll ever be!"

Talking to take his mind off the spinach, endive, kale, and arugula, he asked, "Did you see the ad for Thelma's Film Club? I phoned the number and got a recorded message, of course. Memberships are fifty dollars for the evening show; a hundred for the late-night show — good for a year. Admission tickets are five dollars. Members may buy tickets for guests. The speaker identified himself as Dick Thackeray, manager, but he added that Thelma Thackeray will host the evening shows."

Polly wondered if the idea would go over in Moose County.

"It'll draw from Lockmaster and Bixby Counties chiefly, I'd guess. But there's no doubt it will benefit Pickax restaurants."

Dessert was frozen yogurt with a choice of three toppings. Qwilleran had all three.

"Any news in your exciting life, Qwill?"

He had to consider awhile. "Yum Yum threw up her breakfast . . . Koko staged a three-alarm yowling fit to let me know one of the faucets was dripping . . ."

"How were Thelma's waffles?"

"Good, but rich. You wouldn't have approved . . . The parrots were amusing and strikingly beautiful."

"What was Thelma wearing?"

"A long yellow garment and two armfuls of bracelets — just gold hoops as thin as wire, but lots of them."

"They're called bangle bracelets," Polly said. "Incidentally, I ran into Fran Brodie at the hair salon today, and she said that Thelma has decided jeweled pins and necklaces and bracelets are too flashy for Moose County. She's put them in her bank vault. She'll just wear her tiny diamond ear-studs and diamond-studded sunglasses and bangle bracelets."

Qwilleran huffed into his moustache and wondered, Are they in her bank vault? . . . or on the way to California with the kidnappers?

He was thinking of his theory — that the ransom demand had been for jewels, not cash. Did the kidnappers follow her here from California? Did she give them everything except diamond ear-studs and bangle bracelets? What jewelry would she wear to visit Pop's grave and have dinner at the Boulder House Inn?

He helped Polly remove the dinner appurtenances from the deck, and then they made plans for the following evening: Dinner at Tipsy's Tavern and then an opera on stereo at home. Polly suggested *La Traviata*.

"Are you going to Homer's birthday celebration in the morning, Qwill?"

"Just as an observer," he said.

Qwilleran described the birthday celebration in his personal journal.

Saturday, April 19 — The lobby of the Ittibittiwassee Estates was trimmed with colorful balloons and crowded with city and county officials, local and state media, and Derek Cuttlebrink with his guitar. Residents were restrained behind roping. Everyone was facing the elevator door.

When it opened, out rolled Homer in a wheelchair pushed by his young wife. He was wearing a gold paper crown tilted at a rakish angle. One could tell by the expression on his furrowed face that neither the crown nor the cameras nor the balloons were his own idea. Sorry, Homer; when you become a civic treasure, you give up certain individual rights. When the prolonged applause began to subside, Derek strummed a few chords and sang in a nasal voice to the tune of George M. Cohan's "You're a Grand Old Flag":

> He's a grand old guy with a spark in his eye
> And as bright as the Fourth of July!
> And they say that he's
> Got both his knees
> And still takes his brandy with rye.
> Now he's ninety-nine
> And he's feeling fine.
> And he still takes the curves in high!
> We'll all be here
> Again next year
> To cheer Homer the grand old guy!

They weren't the best lyrics I'd ever written, but Derek made them sound good. As the applause reached a crescendo, the elevator doors opened, the wheelchair rolled back into the car, the door closed, and the green light signaled UP.

CHAPTER
THIRTEEN

The Siamese knew when Qwilleran was getting dressed to go out. They hung around, as only cats can do, waiting, waiting — for a farewell morsel of mozzarella.

He said to them, "I'm taking 'Ducky' for a drive around the county. Sorry you're not invited. She has an aversion to cats." He could understand an allergy to cat hair, but anyone who simply hated cats was suspect.

At Number Five Pleasant Street he was greeted by Thelma, looking handsome in a lime-green jacket of soft leather and a white leather car-cap. A T-shirt in narrow stripes of multi-green and white had a jaunty look. Her slacks, sandals, and satchel-type handbag were white. She was ready to go.

"I forgot to tell you," he said. "We have to walk up a gravel path at Hilltop. Do you have something more practical for walking?"

"No sooner said than done! I'll go up and change, and you say hello to the Amazons while you're waiting."

He could hear them. It sounded like a cocktail party out of control, but the chattering and whooping stopped when he appeared, except for a saucy remark: "Pretty fellow! Pretty fellow!"

"Skip the compliments," Qwilleran said. "Let's hear some intelligent conversation."

There followed a chorus of non sequiturs: "What time is it? . . . Yankee Doodle came to town . . . Yoo Hoo — Yoo Hoo . . . Pretty fellow!"

"They like you," said Thelma, returning in white oxfords with crepe soles. "They don't like everybody."

"I'm flattered," he said.

She hopped nimbly into Qwilleran's SUV.

"Before we push off," he said, "let me congratulate you on the Film Club and wish you success. It will be good for the community, but isn't it an ambitious venture for you?"

"My nephew will do the work and take the responsibility, but the club is in my name, and I'll supervise."

Qwilleran was accustomed to hearing the problems of individuals old and young. They confided in him because he was a good listener and had a sympathetic mien and knew how to say the right thing.

Now he said, "If there's anything I can do, I'll be only too glad to help."

With that they headed north to Hilltop — past the medical center, community college, K Theatre for stage productions, Toodle's Supermarket, curling club in a Swiss chalet, and Ittibittiwassee Estates. They were all new in recent years. "But I remember Lanspeak Department Store," she said. "That's where I went to buy my Easter hat. Hats were always important to me. I don't know why."

"It was your royal instinct. You were born to wear a crown. It shows in your posture, your bearing, your attitude."

"You say the most adorable things, Ducky! I would have loved to be the gossip columnist Hedda Hopper, and be famous for my hats. She had a hundred of them, you know, and she was photographed for the cover of *Time* magazine, wearing a hat composed of a typewriter, a microphone, and a radio script."

"It's interesting that you both happened to have alliterative names."

"Furthermore," he said, "let me say in all sincerity that I think Thelma and Thurston are beautiful names for twins whose surname is Thackeray. Who made the choice?"

"My mother, before we were born. If she had a girl, she wanted her to be Thelma; if she had a boy, he was to be Thurston. In the family, though, we were just Bud and Sis. My father was Pop . . . Did you have brothers and sisters, Qwill?"

"No, and my father died before I was born . . . Were you ever married?"

"Only once. I kicked him out after six months. He was a gambler, and I had no intention of financing his hobby. Since then I've managed very well on my own. As the saying goes: *A woman without a man is like a fish without a bicycle.*"

They drove in silence for a while. Then she said, "Beautiful country." Thelma was relaxed and losing her professional veneer.

"How long did it take you to drive from California?"

"It's about two thousand miles, and we could have made it comfortably in five days; but we didn't want to stress the Amazons, and we didn't want to arrive before the moving van, so we took it slowly, stopping at cabins instead of motels. That way we could take the brood indoors and uncover their cages, and they wouldn't bother anyone. They were good travelers, and Janice is an excellent driver."

After another few minutes of comfortable silence, Qwilleran said, "We're coming to Hilltop — ahead on the left."

The Hilltop Cemetery was in the Hummocks — a ridge running north and south with burial grounds on the summit. The gravestones could be seen silhouetted against the western sky.

Qwilleran said, "Through a member of the genealogy club I was able to check the location of your father's grave. There are five paths leading to the summit. Taking the nearest and walking along the crest produces a mood of healing serenity, they say."

They found the monument to "Milo the Potato Farmer," and Qwilleran wandered away while Thelma had her few moments alone with "Pop".

As they continued toward the shore, Qwilleran said, "Lower your window, Thelma, and sniff the lake air — a hundred miles of water between here and Canada. The Boulder House was originally the summer home of a quarry owner."

The architectural curiosity loomed on a cliff above a sandy beach, looking more like a fortress than a pleasant place for Sunday dinner, and the innkeeper was straight out of a medieval woodcut: short, roly-poly, and leather aproned, but he was jovial, and regular customers affectionately called him "Mine Host".

Before dinner they had a drink on the parapet, a stone veranda over the edge of the cliff, but Thelma said, "I'm not supposed to imbibe, Ducky. Doctor's orders. And at my age I have to be a very good girl."

He recommended a Q cocktail and was explaining about Squunk water when a large, furry animal waddled up to them in a friendly fashion.

"What's that?" she cried in alarm.

"That's Rocky, the resident cat. What you see is mostly fur; he's a longhair, but if you don't want him around, just shoo him away."

When Rocky had retired to the other end of the parapet, Qwilleran told how the craggy design of the building enabled Rocky to climb up the exterior wall like an Alpine goat and peer in the windows at sleeping guests.

Thelma shuddered visibly.

The dining room was equally rough-hewn and the floor was a flat slab of prehistoric rock on which the structure had been built. There was an immense fireplace, screened for the summer.

"In cold weather," Qwilleran said, "guests gather around the fireplace after dinner, and Mine Host tells ghost stories and other hair-raising tales. The menu is not sophisticated, but everything's good."

140

They had a simple Chateaubriand, a twice-baked potato, and what Qwilleran called the inevitable broccoli. After the blueberry cobbler and while they were lingering over coffee, the innkeeper inquired if they had enjoyed the meal.

Qwilleran said, "Ms. Thackeray, this is Silas Dingwall, great-grandson of the man who was responsible for this Eighth Wonder of the World."

"How did he do it?" she exclaimed. "And why?"

"If you'd like to come to my office," said the innkeeper, "it would be my pleasure to serve you an after-dinner drink and tell you the whole story."

They agreed, and Thelma whispered, "Isn't he a character!"

Qwilleran thought, It takes one to know one!

In the office he asked permission to tape the innkeeper's tale, and the following account was recorded:

In the late nineteenth century, when Moose County was booming, the lumber barons built huge summer palaces along the shore here. There was more money than taste in those days — maybe today, too. At any rate, the lumbermen tried to outdo each other, each palace being larger or more spectacular than its neighbors.

My ancestors were in the quarry business and were considered in a lower class than the big boys who were exploiting the mines and forests. But my great-grandfather had a sense of humor, and he and my dad and uncles thought up a crazy idea.

141

They hauled huge boulders to the site and piled them up to make a habitation. It took teams of draft horses and musclemen to do it, and the result has been a tourist attraction ever since.

Then in 1912 the economy collapsed, and people fled the area. The few who remained all but starved until . . . Prohibition went into effect, and a new industry was born. Rumrunners smuggled Canadian whiskey into Moose County, stealthily by night, and bootleggers devised crafty ways to distribute it Down Below. The nerve center of the major operation was a network of subterranean chambers under this building, reached by a tunnel from the beach.

During Silas's tale, Qwilleran watched Thelma for a flickering of eyelids or moistening of lips or any other reflex signifying that she knew about Pop's involvement. There was not even a change in her breathing, and she said coolly, "It would make a good movie . . . with a mysterious tapping in the cellar . . . and the ghost of a revenue agent trapped by a high tide surging into the tunnel."

Entering into the spirit of the scenario, Qwilleran said, "The lakes don't have tides, but it would be a stormtossed surf with thunder and lightning and some wild passages from Tchaikovsky. Boris Karloff could play the ghost!"

He thought, Maybe she didn't make it "in pictures", but she can play a role. Or does she really believe the potato chip story?

Before the day was over, there were more unanswered questions.

They returned to Pickax via the lakeshore, stopping now and then to enjoy the view: sailboats on the horizon . . . cabin cruisers going nowhere fast . . . fishing boats purposefully anchored.

Thelma said, "The lake didn't play any part in our life when we were growing up. We didn't even know it was there."

"What was it like — being a twin? Was there a lot of togetherness?"

"Well, we had different interests, but we were always together in spirit. Each of us had to know where the other was at all times. Although twins, we had very different personalities. Bud was skinny and sensitive; I was husky and tough. Once I bloodied the nose of a bully who was tormenting Bud in the schoolyard. The teacher bawled me out, but I told her I was proud of it and would do it again. After he went east to college and I went west, we kept in touch. I was so proud of him. He was a doctor and had his own animal clinic. He had such a wonderful, caring way with his patients — mostly horses and dogs — and their owners, too. One woman, whose Doberman was not responding to treatment, said she'd like to consult a psychic who diagnosed animals' disorders — by phone! Instead of scoffing at the idea, Bud told her to go ahead and tell him the psychic's diagnosis. He said he might learn something . . . but I'm telling you more than you really want to know."

"On the contrary! I'm sincerely interested. Do you know that you brother's portrait still hangs in the lobby of the clinic he founded? It's a strong countenance. I wish I might have met him. John Bushland took the photo, and he's famous for catching the real person. He'll have the negative. I can get you an eight-by-ten."

"Bless you! Bud used to write me the most beautiful letters, Qwill, and I've saved them, thinking they'd make a heartwarming book for animal lovers. What do you think?"

"I'd have to see them, but I'd be glad to give you an opinion."

"Bud's last letter was so beautiful!" She removed her sunglasses and dabbed her eyes with a tissue.

Then she said, "I'm afraid Dickie Bird is not the man his father was. That's why I'm here. The Film Club, I hope, will give him a challenge and a responsibility."

"Very commendable," Qwilleran murmured, although he considered "Dickie Bird" as a pet name for a male child unsuitable; it would warp a man for life.

He could feel a mood of tension in the seat beside him. He asked, "Are you getting good response to your ad about the Film Club? Moose County has never had such a facility."

Thelma brightened. "Dick reports hundreds of phone calls, and he's selling Gold Memberships for the evening show and Green Memberships for the late show — on credit cards."

"Who's selecting the old movies?"

"That's one responsibility I reserve for myself. I'd be glad to include your requests."

He had never been a film fan, but he remembered *A Tale of Two Cities* and Dickens was one of his favorite storytellers.

When he mentioned the title, Thelma said with enthusiasm, "That's one of my favorites, too! I still choke up when I hear Ronald Colman's last line!"

"Is Dwight Somers doing a good job of P.R. for you?"

"He's one of the best I've ever worked with. Such a pleasant young man. I adore men with beards! And moustaches, too!" she added with a playful nudge.

Qwilleran felt a tremor on his upper lip — not because of the saucy compliment but by a feeling that Dickie Bird smiled too much.

Back on Pleasant Street Qwilleran escorted her to her door but declined a cup of tea, saying he had to go home and feed the cats.

He felt he had done his good-turn-of-the-day, or even of-the-week. Thelma had visited Pop's grave; Janice had been free to go for a cruise. A ploy to bring the potato chip heiress out of the closet had failed, but it was only a journalist's nagging curiosity about something that was none of his business. He admitted it. But Thelma had enjoyed the sightseeing and the Boulder House legend. And she had learned that she could say "shoo" to Rocky and he would oblige. It might be the first step in curing Thelma's ailurophobia.

On arriving at the barn Qwilleran felt the need for a dish of ice cream and some music. He played a Verdi opera that Polly had recently given him, on the barn's magnificent stereo system.

All three of them listened. It was one of the things they could do together as a family. The cats huddled in one comfortable chair, sophisticated enough to take the booming bassos and high-pitched coloraturas without flinching, although their ears twitched once in a while, and occasionally they went to the kitchen for a drink of water.

CHAPTER
FOURTEEN

Qwilleran was leaving to have lunch with Wetherby, the wacky weatherman, and the Siamese were watching as if they knew where he was going. He asked them, "Do you have any message to send to your friend Jet Stream?"

Yum Yum sneezed softly, and Koko felt a sudden urge to scratch his right ear. Why was it always the right?

Wetherby was a native of Lockmaster County who had grown up in the town of Horseradish and had the mind-set and social flair and snappy wardrobe of south-of-the-border types — everything except the two-tone shoes, Qwilleran had observed.

Being the first to arrive at Onoosh's Café, he stood outside to enjoy the pleasant April breeze.

Then, who should come along but Wetherby in black-and-white shoes!

"What happened?" Qwilleran asked in mock sympathy. "Oh! Excuse me. I thought you had an accident and your feet were bandaged."

Unruffled, Wetherby said, "You should get some two-tones, Qwill. They're very big right now."

"My feet are big enough in ordinary shoes, Joe. Shall we go in?"

They sat in a booth and ordered baba ghanouj as an appetizer. (No one had told Qwilleran it was made of egg-plant.)

"How's our friend Jet Stream?" he asked.

"He's a good cat. We're buddies," Wetherby said, "but I spend a fortune on cat litter. The vet says the old boy has a case of 'Gullivarian hydraulics' — nothing serious. But he's aptly named. How are your two brats?"

"They stay busy — Yum Yum rifling wastebaskets, and Koko prowling the bookshelves, sniffing the glue in the bindings. Lately he wants me to read from *Poor Richard's Almanac* all the time, but I get tired of his wit and wisdom."

"Like what?"

"*A man without a wife is only half a man.*"

"Propaganda!" Wetherby objected.

"Prejudiced, to say the least! So I've decided to publish a compendium of wit and wisdom, to be called *Cool Koko's Almanac* with catly sayings."

"Do you happen to remember a couple of examples?"

"*A cat without a tail is better than a politician without a head . . . A cat can look at a king, but he doesn't have to lick his boots . . . Hear no evil, see no evil, speak no evil, but be sure your claws are sharp* . . . But enough of that! What's happening in Indian Village?"

In the winter, when the barn was hard to heat, Qwilleran moved his household to a condo unit next door to Wetherby. It was a good address, but the developer had skimped on construction. Floors bounced; walls between units were thin. Now the K Fund owned Indian Village and improvements were being made. It meant soundproofing the wall between Qwilleran's foyer and Wetherby's living room.

"Amazing what they can do without making a mess," the weatherman said. "They surround the work area with plastic sheeting, then drill holes in the wall and blow in the insulation; cover the holes; paint over them. Neat operation. I thought our studs would be two-by-fours, but luckily they're two-by-sixes, so they could blow in more insulation."

"Is it effective?"

"Since you and your operatic cats aren't in residence — and the unit on the other side of me is for sale — I can't tell. But others in the Village are pleased — even fussbudgets like Amanda Goodwinter! She's mellowed somewhat since being elected mayor. I think its because her P.R. adviser made her get a cat to improve her image."

Amanda had long been the crotchety owner of a successful design studio and a cantankerous member of the town council. No matter how much she spent on clothes and grooming, she always looked like a scarecrow. When it came to getting a cat, her friends expected her to adopt a scruffy orange tom with half a tail and one chewed ear. Instead she acquired a glamourous longhair whom she named Quincy, after an early president of the United States.

"Speaking of cats," Qwilleran said, "are you involved in the Kit Kat Revue?"

"Yeah . . . They asked me to emcee."

Qwilleran said, "I'd better brush up my tap dancing and do a brother-and-sister act with Mayor Goodwinter." Actually he hoped to do a reading of some of T. S. Eliot's madcap verses in *Old Possum's Book of Practical Cats*. He often read them to the Siamese. Yum Yum liked the one about Mungojerrie and Rumpelteazer, who prowled about the house stealing things; she could identify. Koko seemed to feel a kinship with Rum Tum Tugger. *For he will do as he do do and there's no doing anything about it.*

After lunch Qwilleran was walking past the library when he noticed Thelma's green coupé in the parking lot. He went into the building and was surprised to see Janice and one of the volunteers dismantling the exhibit of movie star photographs.

"What's happening?" he asked.

"Oh! It's you!" Janice said. "What a nice surprise! Thelma said everyone has seen the photos and it's time to show some different ones. She's had a new sign made."

It read: EXHIBIT COURTESY OF THELMA'S FILM CLUB.

He said, "I'll buy you a cup of coffee when you've finished the job. Don't hurry."

While waiting, he browsed, said a few words to Mac and Katie, put a dollar in their jar, and bantered with the young clerks at the circulation desk.

"Mrs Duncan is attending a business luncheon," one said. "She didn't say what time she'd be back."

They found their boss's low-key romance with the famous Mr Q to be of extreme interest and they would no doubt find it momentous when he left the building with the new woman from Hollywood, who was younger than Mrs Duncan but not as nice-looking.

He and Janice walked the short distance to Lois's Luncheonette as he explained the cultural significance of the shabby, noisy, friendly eatery; and when they arrived, a political argument was in progress among the customers, with Lois herself refereeing as she walked about swinging the coffee server.

The voices hushed as Mr Q entered with a strange woman. "Come in!" Lois called out. "Sit anywhere! All the tables are clean. Two pieces of apple pie left in the kitchen."

Janice whispered, "Thelma wouldn't care for this place, but I love it!"

"What is Thelma doing this afternoon?" he asked casually.

"Meditating in her Pyramid. She has one made of copper, which concentrates the electronized energy more efficiently. It will do her good. She was upset after an argument with Dick this morning."

"Has he been giving Lolita chocolate caramels again?"

Janice hesitated. "Maybe I shouldn't talk about this, but I worry about her and it helps if I can get another opinion. She's been so good to Dick, and he's so ungrateful."

"You're quite right to be concerned, Janice. Do you know what they were arguing about?"

"Employees for the Film Club. They'll need people to take tickets, run the projector, serve drinks, and clear away between shows. Dick wants to bring in people he knows — from Bixby. Thelma insists on hiring local help — for several good reasons."

"She's entirely right."

"Well, Dick stormed out of the house and slammed the door, so I guess Thelma used her Big Stick. She always talks about carrying a Big Stick to get her own way."

Qwilleran said, "One wonders why Dick was so determined to hire Bixby Bums, as they're called in Moose County." (He thought he knew.)

Changing the subject Qwilleran asked, "How was the boat ride yesterday?"

"Wonderful! The *Viewfinder* is a beautiful cruiser. The Handleys were nice. And the lunch was good. Bushy is a lot of fun. He told stories about his ancestors, who were commercial fishermen, and about UFOs, and about the terrible shipwrecks before the government built the lighthouse."

"And what is the response to the ad for Thelma's Film Club?"

"Very good! Dick is selling both Gold and Green Memberships."

"Has the opening date been decided?" Qwilleran asked casually.

152

"Not definitely. Thelma wants it to coincide with a triple-high on her BioRhythm chart."

He nodded sagely. "A wise approach!"

"And guess who's coming for opening night?"

He thought, It can't be Mr Simmons! Or can it?

"Mr Simmons!" she announced.

"As a friend of the family or a security guard?"

"Just a friend, although Thelma says he has a suspicious eye that roves around and frisks everyone visually." Janice said this with much amusement.

"Is there anything I can do to help during his stay? Pick him up at the airport?"

"Thelma says he'd be very interested in seeing your barn. She told him about it."

"That could be arranged," Qwilleran said genially.

"And Bushy has offered to take us out on the *Viewfinder*."

Janice was far different from the shy guest she had been at the reception. Had Thelma decided it was now "all right" to talk openly with Mr Q? His sympathetic listening always attracted confidences.

Janice was saying, "Bushy is going to do a portrait of Thelma like the one he did of her brother. And she's commissioned him to do still lifes of each of her twenty-four hats — to be made into a book. A woman in California is going to write the text. You haven't seen the hats, have you? I have some snapshots that I took . . ." She rummaged in her handbag.

Qwilleran looked at them and thought, More art than hat! "Interesting," he said.

"Fran Brodie said we should offer them to the Art Center for an exhibit."

Qwilleran said, "There's a gallery opening in Mooseville that would get better traffic and a more sophisticated audience. Tourists come up from Down Below and summer people come over from Grand Island on their yachts. I suggest you show these snapshots to Elizabeth Hart. She's co-owner of the Grist Mill restaurant and founder of Elizabeth's Magic, a boutique in Mooseville. Tell her I said it will get statewide publicity."

Qwilleran was not prepared for the weary "hello" he heard when he phoned Polly for their evening chat.

"Polly! Are you all right?" he asked in alarm.

"I don't know. I'm at sixes and sevens. I had my quarterly luncheon with my friend Shirley — the Lockmaster librarian, you know. It was her turn to drive up here. We went to Onoosh's, which isn't busy on Mondays, and had a booth for privacy. We met to discuss library problems and solutions.

"We compared notes and personal feelings and came to the conclusion that libraries aren't as much fun as they used to be, twenty years ago. Libraries, we said, used to be all about books! And people who read! Now it's all about audios and videos and computers and people in a hurry. What used to be serenely open floor space is now cluttered with everything except books. Even the volunteers find it less attractive work, and stop reporting on schedule.

"The public flocks in to see movie stars' photos, but no one shows up for a book program. Shirley's quitting! Her son owns the bookstore in Lockmaster, and she's going to work there. I planned to continue, but can I stand another five years of frustration? And if I leave, what will I DO? I could teach adults to read . . . or do you have any suggestions, Qwill?"

Qwilleran said calmly, "If the K Fund opened a bookstore in Pickax, Polly, would you manage it?"

"What! You don't mean it!" she cried.

"It's a crime for a community of this size to have no bookstore! You could have book reviews, discussion groups, and readings from the classics . . . a busload could come in from Ittibittiwassee Estates."

Polly said, "I think I'm going to faint!"

Qwilleran said, "Before you pass out, let me thank you for the opera recording!"

CHAPTER
FIFTEEN

Qwilleran was serious about the bookstore. There would be long meetings with G. Allen Barter, attorney for the K Fund, and trips to Chicago for Polly's decisions: whether to build a new store on Book Alley or adapt the premises of the old *Pickax Picayune*. Meanwhile there would be the Kit Kat Revue to produce . . . and Thelma's Film Club to launch, and another Tuesday deadline for the "Qwill Pen."

Qwilleran was polishing his thousand words on *Cool Koko's Almanac* when Thornton Haggis phoned. "I have some interesting news for you, Qwill. Are you free?"

"I'm on deadline. Why don't you come up at two o'clock? Bring my mail and newspaper, and we'll have some refreshments. Will your news keep?"

"It's kept for a century. Another few hours won't hurt. It's something I heard at the genealogical society last night."

That lessened the newsman's anticipation somewhat but he said, "I can hardly wait!"

After two o'clock his friend Thorn trudged up the lane from the Art Center, and Qwilleran met him with a pitcher of sangria. They discussed the weather, the future of Thelma's Film Club, and the price of gasoline. Then Qwilleran asked about the G.S., as the ten-syllable organization was popularly called.

"Well . . . a couple of years ago they started an inventory of lost cemeteries."

"How does a cemetery get lost?"

"Starting about 1850, people were buried in backyards and along roadsides and in tiny churchyards. There is no trace of them today, but a group of G.S. members who call themselves grave-finders have searched county records and found hundreds of names and scores of old cemetery locations. Most of the little churches have been destroyed, but they found one small log church about the size of a one-car garage but with a proud little steeple. A stone wall surrounds a small graveyard with headstones no bigger than a concrete block — but with names and dates. The oldest is 1918. But it's completely overgrown. In fact, it's now part of a Klingenschoen Conservancy. The G.S. is getting permission to clear it out as a historic site. But here's the surprise! Three Thackerays are buried there, and they're pretty sure that Milo and some other farmers built the church."

"Hmmm," Qwilleran mused. "It would make a good story for the *Something* if handled right. Does the G.S. have any plans?"

"Since the last of the Moose County Thackerays has returned, they thought some kind of dedication ceremony might be in order. You know her; do you think she'd go for that?"

"She likes publicity, if it's favorable. She's hired a P.R. consultant. I could sound her out."

"We won't release the news of the Thackeray graves until we hear from you, Qwill."

Qwilleran had promised to take Thelma to lunch at the Nutcracker Inn; he could combine it with a sightseeing drive around the county, including the Old Log Church. After Thornton's visit, he phoned her, and before he could extend his invitation, she cried, "Bless you, Ducky, for sending us to that talented Elizabeth Hart! She came down this morning to see our hats, and she said she'll be thrilled to exhibit them!"

"I want to hear all about it! Suppose I pick you up at eleven tomorrow morning — for lunch and sightseeing."

"What kind of shoes shall I wear?" was her prompt reply.

He hung up with the satisfaction of "mission accomplished."

Before the day was over, he would have a harder task.

The Kit Kat system of foster care for kittens, which was new to Moose County, had been quietly succeeding, and now it was time to go public with a fund-raising Kit Kat Revue. The question was: When and where? A problem-solving session at the MacLeod residence on Pleasant Street was scheduled for Tuesday evening. Qwilleran walked over there at seven-thirty as several neighbors were converging on the site, and a carload drove in from Indian Village. Hannah MacLeod greeted everyone at the door, while Uncle Louie MacLeod sat at the baby grand and played numbers from the musical *Cats*.

The house had been occupied by three generations of musical MacLeods and was filled with family heirlooms and family portraits of opera singers, violinists, and pianists.

The newest member of the family — the recently adopted Danny — escorted guests to the adjoining family room with the official zeal of an eight-year-old. He brought extra chairs from the dining room, asked if anyone wanted a drink of bottled water, and answered questions about the kitten colonies.

"They have to stay with their mother for eight weeks . . . She feeds them and shows them how to take a bath . . . She picks them up by the back of the neck and drops them in their sandbox. She teaches them how to play."

When the last guest had arrived — Burgess Campbell with Alexander — Uncle Louie played a few chords of "God Bless America" and Danny said, "Everybody stand up and sing!"

The meeting was chaired by Mavis Adams, instigator of the local foster-care program and promoter of the fund-raising revue. She introduced two special guests. Hixie Rice was promotion director at the *Moose County Something*, which would underwrite expenses of the revue as a public service. Dwight Somers was the public-relations consultant who would advise the Kit Kat Revue committee pro bono.

Mavis said, "We have our program material well in hand, but we can't decide on staging or the price of tickets until we know the when-and-where of the revue."

Burgess Campbell spoke up. "May I say that this county has plenty of affluent individuals who will support a good cause if the event has an element of novelty and exclusivity. Fifty persons paid three hundred dollars a ticket for a black-tie cheese-tasting . . . chiefly because it was held at Qwill's barn. The renovated opera house would be a similar drawing card while it's hot news."

Uncle Louie asked, "Would the old gal let us borrow it for one night? She's said to hate cats. What does Somers & Beard have to say about this?"

"She's highly sensitive about her image," the P.R. man said. "In a county of ten thousand cat-fanciers I'd advise against the ailurophobe label. But since I'm working for her, I can't be a special pleader for the Kit Kat Revue. You'll have to request the use of the opera house. Then, if she asks my opinion — which she will — I'll endorse it."

Wetherby said, "Qwill's in solid with Thelma. I move that we appoint him special pleader."

"Seconded!"

"All in favor?"

Every hand was raised.

Uncle Louie asked, "Has anyone seen the hall?"

"It seats about a hundred cabaret-style, at small round tables," Dwight said. "There's stage, with a full-size movie screen for a backdrop. There's a bar for serving beverages. Plenty of space backstage."

Someone asked, "Does anyone know how they've decorated the interior of the opera house?"

Only Dwight had seen it. "Everything's a grayish purple like an ophthalmologist's waiting room — not too dark, not too light. The tables are small and round and pedestal-type. The chairs swivel and roll on casters and are quite comfortably upholstered."

There was excited babble in the room, and Mavis rapped for attention, and asked Uncle Louie for an update on the program.

He said, "Besides musical numbers and humorous readings, there will be performances by the creative dance club at the school and the tumbling team wearing cat costumes with tails. The kids visited several foster-care colonies to get ideas about kittens at play."

Then Hixie Rice asked to have the floor. "I would like to suggest a rousing finale for the program: a procession across the stage of prominent citizens with their cats! The mayor, the superintendent of schools, the director of the public library, newspaper personalities, and our esteemed meteorologist, of course." There were cheers, and Wetherby took a bow.

Hixie went on. "I know where I can order rhinestone-studded harnesses and leashes — overnight delivery — for marching across the stage."

A commanding voice said, "May I say a few words?"

All heads turned to listen. Qwilleran was not only *who he was*, but the "Qwill Pen" column had made him an authority on feline eccentricities. He said, "A cat may walk on a leash in a park, stopping to sniff an unidentified object or to chase a blowing leaf. But will he walk in a straight line — from stage-left to stage-right — in front of a hundred strangers?"

All heads turned to Hixie. "If they won't walk, they can be carried or wheeled in some kind of conveyance. Also, there is a safe herbal sedation that's used in the theatre when a cat plays a role in a play — Pywacket in *Bell, Book and Candle,* for example. It produces serenity."

"In the actors or the cat?" Wetherby asked.

Mavis said, "We can cross that bridge when we come to it."

And Uncle Louie said, "Everything depends on whether Qwill can twist Thelma's arm."

"Hear! Hear!" everyone shouted, and the meeting was adjourned.

Back at the barn, Koko was doing his grasshopper act.

"Were your ears burning?" Qwilleran asked. "How are you going to feel about a rhinestone-studded harness?"

But no. The cat was announcing a message on the answering machine — from Bushy.

"Would you like to earn a little extra money Thursday morning? Call me back."

Qwilleran phoned him. "Doing what?"

"Photographer's assistant. No experience necessary. Easy work. Low pay. I'm shooting all twenty-four of Thelma's hats, and it would speed matters if someone held the lights."

"Don't you have light stands?"

"Frankly," Bushy said, "the two gals will be hanging around and wanting to talk, and you can shoo them away diplomatically."

"Okay, but give my remuneration to charity. I don't want to report it to the IRS."

"I'll pick you up Thursday morning."

Qwilleran liked the idea. He had promised Thelma lunch at the Nutcracker Inn; news about the Old Log Church suggested a nostalgic trip to her distant past; and helping Bushy shoot the hats would be another point in his favor before "popping the question."

CHAPTER
SIXTEEN

When Qwilleran called for Thelma on Wednesday morning, Janice came to the door and said, "Come in. She's all ready. She's just saying good-bye to the Amazons. Do you say good-bye to your cats?" she asked.

"Always," said Qwilleran.

Thelma arrived in such a flurry of enthusiasm and anticipation that Qwilleran was aware only that she was wearing something lavender and bangle bracelets and diamond ear-studs and crepe-soled shoes.

She hopped into the SUV with the pep of a twenty-year-old and asked, "Are we going anywhere near Toodle's Market?"

"In Moose County everything is near everything else. Why do you ask?"

"Janice buys our groceries there and raves about it. Also, the woman who runs it is called Grandma Toodle, and she says she knows me from grade school."

"Then that will be our first stop."

They found Grandma Toodle in the produce department sniffing pineapples critically. She looked up and flung her arms wide. "Thelma! I saw your picture in the paper! Do you remember me? Emma Springer! You called me your little sister."

"You were so tiny! I had to look after you. You had beautiful long curls, and when the boys pulled them, I chased them with a big stick."

"And now you're famous, Thelma!"

"I still carry a 'big stick'!"

Qwilleran wandered away and inspected the broccoli until the hysterical reunion ended.

Thelma bought a fresh pineapple, explaining that it contained an enzyme that would cure what ails you. Qwilleran bought some eating apples, and they joined the lineup at the checkout counter. There was a wait, as usual, while a customer searched for her credit card and the cashier had to find out today's price of bananas. In front of Thelma a boy of about ten years waited patiently as his mother complained about the holdup; he was eating candy out of a paper bag.

Suddenly he turned to Thelma and said, "Would you like a jelly bean?" He offered the bag to the customer with diamond ear-studs and bangle bracelets.

"Thank you, Ducky!" she said. "Do you have any black ones?"

"Yep, but you have to dig for 'em."

Thelma reached into the bag just as the boy's mother said, "Don't eat all that candy, Jason. You'll spoil your dinner." And the line moved up a few inches.

"Nice young boy," Thelma remarked as they left the market.

"Did you find a black one?" he asked.

"After he'd been digging around with his grubby hands? I took one for Lolita. She doesn't care what color it is."

As they drove away, her musings rambled. "Just imagine! — little Emma Springer marrying big Buck Toodle! We all went to a two-room school! Eight grades with one teacher and a potbellied stove!"

Qwilleran asked, "Did you write secret messages to each other with lemon juice?"

"Are you kidding, Ducky? I never saw a lemon until I moved to California! . . . The Toodles had a crossroads grocery, with everything from turnips to kerosene. We had to walk a mile to spend a penny on candy. We walked everywhere, except in blizzards. We'd put on our Sunday best and walk to church and arrive covered with dust . . . I liked going to church because I could wear a hat . . . Always loved headgear. I paraded around the house with pots and pans on my head. I made hats out of cornflake boxes."

"Do you remember the name of your church?"

"No, but it was built of huge logs. Pop helped to build it. He said it would last forever."

"He may have been right. The forest grew up around it, but it's being cleared out, and a friend told me how to find it. It has a little graveyard with a stone wall around it."

Farther on, an arrow pointed to THE OLD LOG CHURCH, and their vehicle bounced down a narrow rutted road through deep woods.

166

At a jog in the road Thelma cried, "That's it! That's it!" She jumped out of the car and knew exactly where to find the three Thackeray graves.

Qwilleran waited until her emotions were played out, then said, "They're planning a dedication ceremony. Would you represent the Thackeray family?"

"Bless you! I'd be honored!"

Back on the pavement they jabbered all the way to the Nutcracker Inn.

He said, "I've bought a Gold Card Membership."

"You shouldn't have, Ducky. You can see a show anytime as my guest."

"But I wanted to be a member. How will we know what's being shown?"

"Members get a newsletter every two months." She mentioned productions like *The African Queen* . . . *The Godfather* . . . *My Fair Lady* . . . *Close Encounters of the Third Kind*. And then, "I've been wondering, Qwill, how you handle the housecleaning in your huge barn."

"Three young men with vacuums and other cleaning equipment come in on a regular schedule, plus an older woman who does dusting and polishing and is very fussy . . . By the way, I'm helping Bushy shoot your hats tomorrow morning."

"Glad you told me! We'll have waffles."

"Not this time. It's strictly a work session. But we'll take a rain check . . . Did the hats make the cross-country trip without damage?"

"Well, each hat has its own sturdy hatbox, and the moving company built four wooden crates that would be a tight fit for six boxes. They were painted THIS SIDE UP in big letters. Perfect!"

The Nutcracker Inn was an old Victorian mansion with a turret and black walnut woodwork, purchased by the K Fund and converted into a stylish resort. Peanuts were supplied for feeding the squirrels that enlivened the extensive grounds, and bread was available for feeding the ducks that paddled about the Black Creek. Qwilleran's old friend, innkeeper Lori Bamba, gave Thelma the kind of effusive welcome she liked. The sleek black Nicodemus, the resident cat, looked on, knowing when and when not to be friendly. Qwilleran noted that Thelma took him in her stride.

Their table was reserved in the conservatory, but first they had Q cocktails on the deck, where they could watch the squirrel ballet.

Qwilleran asked, "What did you think about the black cat?"

"He has wicked eyes," she replied noncommittally.

"But a sweet disposition. In fact, guests who are lonesome for their pets can arrange for him to stay overnight with them. In fact, he's reserved far in advance." The latter was a little hyperbole added for comic effect, and Thelma looked at him sharply. He went on. "How do you feel about cats? I was told to keep mine out of sight when you were coming."

"I'm not enthusiastic."

"We had all kinds of barn cats on the farm, and they adored my brother. He had a kind of magnetism, even then, that attracted cats and dogs. I was jealous I think.

I pulled their tails and one of Bud's cats bit me. They were the only thing he and I ever fought about . . . After he was a doctor — and we kept in constant touch — cats were never mentioned."

Qwilleran nodded sympathetically. "But that was then, and this is now. You're living in a community where there are one-point-five cats for every person. We all have our likes and dislikes. Still, there are busybodies who are spreading the rumor that you're a 'cat hater'. Now is the time to make some gesture that will squelch the rumor. You might consult Dwight Somers. And who's your local attorney?" He knew, but he wanted to hear it from her.

Thelma brightened. "Mavis Adams! First woman attorney I've ever had. She's a gem! She listens; she understands; she gives good advice; she solves problems."

Qwilleran added, "And she lives on Pleasant Street. It wouldn't hurt to discuss the matter with her. She founded the local chapter of an animal-rescue movement and is spearheading a revue to raise funds for it. Whatever amount is realized, the K Fund will match dollar-for-dollar."

The hostess interrupted to say their table was ready, and they went into the conservatory. It was a many-windowed room with views on three sides.

Thelma said, "Pop built one of these on the back of the farmhouse after he did well in potato chips. We called it a sun parlor."

After they had ordered (roast beef sandwich for him, something patently healthful for her), he brought up the subject of Bud's letters. "Do you still want an opinion as to their possible publication?"

"I do! I do! Janice is putting them in chronological order and then in letter files for your convenience. She's such a joy! — an efficient secretary, wonderful cook, and careful driver! Off the record, Qwill, I've set up a trust fund for her future financial needs. And now that we're living here, I hope she will make some friends. She goes over to the Campbell house to play with the kittens, and that's good for her."

After lunch they walked down the hill to the creek, carrying some bread to feed to the ducks. They sat on a park bench facing the water, and immediately two mother ducks and their broods sailed toward them in perfect formation. Thelma was delighted with the performance, and after the bread was gone, she was reluctant to leave.

"It's so peaceful here," she said. Then, after a long pause, she asked suddenly, "Do you think I was right to start Thelma's Film Club?"

"It seems like a great idea to me, Thelma. And you say the memberships are selling well. Are there problems?"

"Only one. My nephew! He's not the man his father was. He wants to have Bingo at the club one night a week! I told him in no uncertain terms that I would not allow gambling in a club with my name on the marquee. He said, 'It's only a game, Auntie.' It irritates me when he calls me that! If it's not gambling, why is it outlawed in so many communities . . . and in places where it's considered legalized gambling, why are there so many restrictions and regulations?"

"You're quite right, Thelma, to limit a film club to films. There's a gambling casino in Bixby County, but Lockmaster and Moose Counties have never permitted it. Was that the end of it?"

"He said we're a private club and can do anything we want — even strip dancing! — as long as it's undercover. I said, 'I'll hear no more of this twaddle! Decide whether you want to work for me — or not!' So he backed down. He knows which side his bread is buttered on!"

"I'm glad to see you stick to your guns, Thelma."

"I *always* stick to my guns."

"When do you start showing films?"

"One week from today. Everything was going so well until the upsetting argument with my nephew."

"Forget about Dickie Bird and what a bad boy he is," said Qwilleran. "Do something constructive that will cancel out your negative feelings! Make a spectacular gesture that will win the admiration of the county."

The rest of their conversation is best reported in Qwilleran's own words — in his personal journal:

Wednesday, April 23 — All during our nostalgia trip around the county and our pleasant luncheon at the Nutcracker Inn, I had been waiting for the right moment to pop the question (as Dwight phrased it). This might be it. I knew she appreciated my hospitality, but I didn't want to ask a favor in return. It would have the taint of *quid pro quo*.

Now she was disenchanted with her nephew and dispirited about the Film Club. I thought fast. The trick would be to boost her morale and solve the Kit Kat problem with one stroke. I said, "I know the situation is disappointing, Thelma, but you must rise above it! Do something constructive that will benefit others as well as yourself!"

Thelma regarded me questioningly, and I went on. "Restoring the old opera house is a boon to the whole county! Even people who aren't interested in old movies are curious to know what you've done with the building. And it so happens that we have plenty of affluent citizens who would pay to have a private look at the building if it would benefit a local charity. (Tax deductible, by the way.) They like to put on dinner jackets and long dresses and be treated like celebrities: valet parking, red carpet, press photographers, even TV cameras from Down Below, and publicity all over the state."

I was on my soapbox, as Polly calls it. Thelma was mesmerized, if I do say so myself. She asked, "Do you mean I should open the theatre for a charity preview? Did you have a charity in mind?"

I said, "Mavis Adams is doing a commendable job of spearheading a new kind of animal-rescue effort and has been rehearsing an entertainment to raise funds. Civic leaders will pay two or three hundred dollars a ticket if it's presented in an environment like the Film Club, and for you to offer the premises would be a handsome gesture. Ask Mavis for details, and consult your P.R. man. I'm sure Dwight will applaud your suggestion."

She said, "I have an appointment with Mavis at the law office tomorrow. I'll mention it . . . It might be an interesting thing to do." Mission accomplished! With no arm-twisting!

But I have a hunch that Dickie Bird is going to be more of a problem than his "auntie" expects.

CHAPTER
SEVENTEEN

On Thursday morning three young men with high-tech cleaning equipment and Mrs Fulgrove with homemade metal polish arrived at the barn, and that meant removing the Siamese from the premises. They wouldn't bother the cleaning crew, but the crew would bother them. Qwilleran put them in the SUV along with their blue cushion, commode, water dish, and snack bowl, and off they went to Pleasant Street to help photograph hats.

Janice met Qwilleran and said, "Bushy's upstairs; Thelma had an appointment with her attorney. Is there anything I can do for you? Coffee? Cold drink?"

"You might like to go out to the car and say hello to the Siamese."

"They could come indoors, since Thelma isn't here."

"No, thanks. They're happy where they are. They have all the comforts of home."

Bushy was in the upstairs room called the Gallery of Hats, setting up. The two side walls had hats displayed on shelves. Others on pedestals were spaced in the middle of the room. Each hat had its own acrylic hat stand.

"Here's what we'll do," he said. "Move all the hats to one side of the room; then move them to the other side one-by-one as they're photographed. That way we won't shoot one hat twice."

Qwilleran said, "That reminds me of the story about the man who wanted some new trousers shortened three inches, and the tailor shortened one leg twice."

"Funny, but I don't have time to laugh. Too much to do." Bushy had set up one pedestal, as a stage for the hat to be photographed. Two floor-standing lights were placed to bounce light off walls and ceiling. The camera was placed on its tripod, ready to go. It would be Qwilleran's job to place a hat on the pedestal and rotate it this way and that until Bushy had the best angle. Then he would tell his assistant how to direct the handheld light to best advantage. "Raise it . . . tilt it down . . . a little to the left . . . move it an inch." The tricky ritual would be repeated three times for each hat.

The first two shots were interesting; after that Qwilleran entertained himself by inventing names for them: Heavenly Hash . . . Chef's Salad . . . Crème de Chocolat. Despite his talent for description, he would find it impossible to do justice to creations like these. There were wisps of this and swirls of that, unexpected trims, touches of hand-painting or stitchery, defiant color contrasts, crowns and brims in mad shapes.

Halfway through, the photographer said, "See if you can scare up some coffee, Qwill, and let's take a breather."

"How do you want it?"

"Naked."

"What do you think of the hats?"

"Well . . . they're different! Wonder what she paid for them?"

"Did you notice the hatboxes?"

Stacked in the corners of the room were two dozen round hatboxes covered in shiny alligator-print paper.

Qwilleran asked about them when he went downstairs for coffee.

"Thelma had them custom-made," Janice said. "She adores the alligator look. She has alligator shoes and handbags."

"Did you go out to see the Siamese?"

"Yes, and I took them a little treat. I also put a couple of boxes of letters from Thelma's brother in the car. I went through them and put them in chronological order to make it easier for you."

"I appreciate that."

Upstairs he told Bushy, "I'll look forward to seeing your prints. You always make everything look better than it is."

"Did Thelma tell you I'm going to do a portrait of her? It'll be a companion to the one hanging in the lobby of the clinic."

"You spoke highly of Dr Thurston, but I don't think you knew much about the son did you?"

"Only by reputation. My ex-wife was a native of Lockmaster, and she said he was a drifter. But he always seemed to have money."

After his dubious experience with twenty-four hats, Qwilleran would have relished a Reuben sandwich and fries at Rennie's, but the Siamese had been confined long enough so he drove back to the barn. His passengers seemed to be peacefully aware of their destination until they entered the deep woods leading to the barnyard. Then a low rumble in Koko's innards became a growl. It was a familiar expression of disapproval. The cleaning crew had gone. There was something indoors that aroused Koko's resentment.

Leaving the cats in the car, Qwilleran let himself into the barn cautiously. There was the reassuring aroma of cleaning fluid and metal polish. And on the bar was a gift-wrapped package — also a scrawled note in the unique style of Mrs Fulgrove: "A man brung this gift which he left no name."

It was wrapped in alligator gift wrap with gauzy black ribbon, and a note from Thelma: "With much thanks for everything; Dick is here and will drop this off at your barn." The box contained a pair of glazed porcelain parrots in brilliant green with patches of red and yellow.

He put them on the mantel beak-to-beak, like Lolita and Carlotta gossiping in Thelma's aviary.

When the Siamese were brought into the barn and released from the carrying coop, Yum Yum emerged timidly as if she had never been there before, but Koko rushed forth, growling and looking in all directions.

Qwilleran slapped his forehead as the situation became clear. Dick Thackeray had delivered the gift. There was something about Thelma's nephew that Koko found repugnant, and he had sensed his presence before they even reached the barnyard. Likewise, after the champagne reception, Koko had entered the barn snarling — snarling at someone who had been there.

Qwilleran opened a can of smoked oysters, which he diced and spread on two plates.

He was led to wonder if Koko's unfriendly performances corroborated Thelma's outpourings on the park bench at Black Creek. And did they explain the cat's choice of books to push off the shelf?

There was always the possibility, of course, that Koko simply enjoyed dislodging a book and seeing it land on the floor with a *thlunk*! The fact that one was *Poor Richard's Almanac* and the other was *Richard Carvel* might be coincidental. Only one thing was sure. Koko had a passion for smoked oysters. He and Yum Yum retired to the blue cushion on the refrigerator and went to sleep.

Now Qwilleran went to the gazebo with a cheese sandwich and a thermos of coffee and the boxes of letters Janice had put in the van. The cordless phone was purposely left indoors.

Thelma's brother was indeed a good writer, but content was more important. The question was: Were they worthy of publication? They spanned thirty-odd years. Bud had married another graduate veterinarian, Dr Sally, and Pop had set them up in a clinic in Lockmaster. But their greatest joy, it seemed, was their son, Dickie Bird — all the more so because Sally would never be able to have another child. They were enthusiastic about their work. They believed in holistic medicine. Sally was taking a course in acupuncture. Their hobbies were music and hiking. Bud played the flute. Every Sunday they left Dickie Bird with his nanny, and they hiked along the rim of the Black Creek Gorge. Bud's descriptions of the gorge bordered on the poetic. They would sit on a large flat rock and eat energy bars and drink bottled water from their knapsacks.

Dickie Bird, as his parents called him privately, was a handsome boy with a genuine likable personality. He did very well in school, played a little tennis, and was popular with classmates, but he showed no interest in hiking. In high school he preferred the company of his own friends.

Bud wrote, "Dick has a talent for living beyond his allowance, but we indulge him. He's our only son! And we know he's not into drugs or anything like that. The kids he runs with are all achievers, with plans for professional careers. Dick hasn't decided what he wants to do. He's old enough to drive now, and we're giving him a car for his birthday . . . Sis, do you remember when Pop gave us a movie palace for our birthday?"

Qwilleran's reading was interrupted by a high-decibel howl from the barn. He raced indoors and found Koko prancing in front of the answering machine. The message was an indignant complaint: "Qwill! Where are you? It's seven o'clock! You were to be here at six!"

"Uh-oh! I'm in the doghouse!" he said to Koko.

The situation was that Polly was in Chicago, and Mildred was in Duluth, and Arch was grilling two porterhouse steaks for a bachelor supper on the deck. Qwilleran thought fast and phoned Wetherby, who lived a city block from the Rikers. It was a long shot, but luckily Wetherby was at home.

"Joe! Do me a favor!" he said with desperation in his voice. "Run — don't walk — to the Rikers' condo and tell Arch you're there to eat my steak. No explanation! No apology! Just tell him I called from the jail."

Qwilleran chuckled. He and Arch, in their lifetime of friendship, had survived many a gaffe, bluff, and tiff — with all systems intact.

Now the phone rang and — thinking it was Arch again — he let the machine pick up the message. It was Hixie Rice, calling from the news office.

Returning her call, Qwilleran listened to her exuberant announcement. "Qwill! We're getting the opera house for the revue! Next Tuesday! Tickets are going to be two hundred! Isn't that thrilling! I told Mavis I'd notify you. Also, Doug Bethune is printing the programs, so he needs to know the titles of the readings you're going to do."

Hixie stopped for breath, and Qwilleran asked the unwise question: "Is there anything I can do?"

"I could really use your input on the subject of the Grand March, Qwill, and the sooner the better. If you could hop up here to the office —"

"If you could hop down here to the barn," he interrupted, "I could offer you a drink."

Hixie Rice was an attractive, spirited woman of unguessable age who was unlucky in love. Qwilleran had first met her Down Below and had followed her exploits like the segments of a soap opera. In the business world, though, her infectious enthusiasm and bright ideas made her a success even when her ideas failed. Qwilleran was always glad to see her.

She arrived at the barn in what Moose Countians would call "two shakes of a lamb's tail." "Where are those adorable cats?" she asked, and they came out to greet her. Everyone liked Hixie.

"What will you have to drink?" Qwilleran asked.

"What are you having?"

"A Q cocktail."

"I'll have a martini."

When they settled into the "seductive" sofas (Hixie's word for them), Qwilleran asked, "How successful have you been in lining up prominent citizens for the finale?"

"Everyone's cooperating!" she said with her usual exuberance. "How does this sound? Newspaper columnist, meteorologist, innkeeper, superintendent of schools, prize-winning woodcrafter, a medical doctor, director of the public library, food editor, two professors (retired), and . . . Her Honor, the mayor! The professors are the Cavendish sisters. Jennie is confined to a wheelchair, so she'll ride with two cats in her lap and Ruth will push."

"Have the rhinestone harnesses been ordered?"

"They're on the way."

"May I refresh your drink?"

She wriggled to get out of the deep-cushioned sofa. "No thanks, but you mix a superb martini! What's your secret?"

"Fourteen to one." Actually he had no dry vermouth, so it was fourteen to zero!

Later that evening, when he phoned Polly in Chicago, he told her about the rhinestone harnesses, the impressive lineup of prominent citizens, and the harmless herbal sedative that would keep the cats calm.

"Oh dear!" she said. "It sounds like another of Hixie's bright ideas! I hope it all works."

"Are your conferences progressing well?"

"We've brainstormed, that's all. We toss out whatever enters our heads. It's quite fun. The K Fund people are charming, and there's been much wining and dining. I'll be glad to get home to an egg salad sandwich. Happily, I'll be leaving Saturday morning and arriving on the noon shuttle flight . . . And I'm bringing you something!"

"What?"

"Wait and see! . . . *A bientôt!*"

"*A bientôt*," he mumbled. He objected to being on the dark side of a secret.

CHAPTER
EIGHTEEN

On Friday morning Qwilleran filed his copy earlier than usual, leading the managing editor to say, "Is something wrong? Or are you a better person from eating all that broccoli?"

"I have other work to do, Junior! And don't you dare touch a single comma in my copy! After last week's proverb fiasco —"

"I know! I know!" Junior threw up both hands in defense.

The truth was that Qwilleran had an urgent desire to return to Thelma's letters from Bud. A familiar sensation in his upper lip was the forerunner of suspicion, corroborated by Koko's growling and spitting at someone or something that was not present. Qwilleran was convinced that it was Dick who was on what he called "Koko's spit list."

First there were errands to do, however, like mailing a letter to England and cashing a check for daily needs.

At the bank Qwilleran found himself in line behind Wetherby. He leaned forward and said quietly, "Has WPKX started paying you for your services?"

The weatherman turned quickly. "Hey! Qwill! That was the best steak I ever ate in my life! I'll understudy you any old time!!"

"Have you time for coffee at Lois's?"

"Next!" the teller said impatiently.

After their transactions were completed, the two men walked to Lois's the long way, in order to see what was happening to the opera house. The old stone building was looking noble once more. The boardings had been taken down. There were new doors. At one side of the entrance a carved wood plaque of tasteful size announced THELMA'S FILM CLUB with letters highlighted in gold. The parking lots on either side were freshly paved. And across the street a strip of storefronts was upgraded. Gone were the plumbing fixtures and printshop clutter. An ice-cream bar, antique shop, and gift gallery were moving in. In the center of the row the door leading to the small apartments upstairs was newly lettered: OPERA HOUSE TERRACE.

Wetherby said, "They're not bad apartments. I visited someone there once. One-bedroom. There's a little upstairs porch all along the back, but good only for raising tomato plants."

"Have you joined the club?" Qwilleran asked.

"Nah. I'm not into old movies. Did you?"

"Only so I can take guests once in a while. I hear that Thelma's nephew is managing it."

"Lots a luck," Wetherby said.

At Lois's they ordered coffee and whatever was freshly baked. It proved to be cinnamon sticky buns.

The implied sneer in Wetherby's last remark supported Qwilleran's growing disenchantment.

He said, "Did I detect a note of cynicism in your remark about Dick Thackeray?"

"Well . . . you know . . . we were in school together all the way through twelfth grade. Us kids from the Village of Horseradish attended a consolidated school in East Lockmaster — a bunch of country bumpkins among all those rich dudes. I knew Dick when we were pitching pennies in the schoolyard. He always won. In high school I had to work hard to get a B; Dick got all A's. I acted in plays; he hung out with eggheads who were going to be scientists. My sport was track; theirs was playing cards — for money. I had to work my way through college; Dick thought college wasn't necessary; he went traveling. Never did settle down to a career. How long is he going to act as manager of his aunt's Film Club?"

"I see what you mean," Qwilleran said.

Then they talked about the Kit Kat Revue; how the cats would get along backstage while waiting to go on . . . what kind of music should be played for the Grand March . . . what Jet Stream and Koko would think about rhinestone harnesses.

Wetherby said, "Well, we'll get a few answers at the rehearsal Monday night."

The Siamese were waiting anxiously at the barn, knowing their noontime snack was eleven minutes late. Qwilleran fed them and even read a passage from the *Wilson Quarterly* aloud — to make them drowsy. After they had crawled away to some secret nap-nook, Qwilleran took a large dish of ice cream to the gazebo, along with the second box of Thackeray letters.

Bud's letters continued infrequently as he grew older. Most of them recounted unusual cases he and Sally treated in their clinic — a veritable name-dropping of famous race-horses and the winners of dog shows. Once there had been a terrible barn fire, and Bud agonized with the owners. Occasionally Dick would arrive unexpectedly and stay for a week. His ingratiating smile and happy disposition always made him a welcome visitor. Sometimes he had a clever idea for a new business venture and they gladly lent him money, although experience had taught them that it would never be returned but that was all right. He was their only son. What better investment could they make? It was too bad he never wanted to go on a nature walk along the Black Creek Gorge.

Then Sally began to slow down, have bad days, stay home from the clinic. During this period investors offered to buy the clinic and relieve him of a burdensome responsibility. After all, he was in his late seventies. But Sally urged him to keep the clinic that had meant so much to him. Dick came and went. Then Sally just faded away. That was all he had the heart to say. He no longer walked along the gorge. But he was thankful that he had his challenging work — and the health to carry on.

That was the last letter in the box. What had happened to the final letter that Thelma called so beautiful? He phoned the Thackeray house, and Janice

186

answered. Thelma was at the club, she said, working out details.

"I've read the two boxes of letters," Qwilleran said, "and the last one seems to be missing."

"Oh! . . . That's right! She keeps it close by so she can read it. It's getting quite worn from all the folding and unfolding."

"You should make a photocopy and preserve the original in some special way. Do you have a copier?"

"No, but I could have it done somewhere in town."

"I have a copier. If you can find the letter, you could bring it over here, and the job could be done in . . . no time." He congratulated himself for avoiding the Moose County cliché."

Soon the green coupé drove into the barnyard, and he took the cherished letter to his studio for copying while Janice talked to the Siamese and looked at titles on the bookshelf.

"This is a funny title," she said when Qwilleran came down the ramp. She was looking at *How to Read a Book* by Dr Mortimer Adler. "If you can read a book on how-to-read-a-book," she said, "why do you need to read this book?"

"Some day I'll lend it to you, and you'll find out . . . I made two copies of the letter and will put one in the box with the others. You can have the other to save wear and tear on the original. Do you have time for a glass of fruit juice?"

He was glad she declined the invitation. He wanted to read Bud's last letter.

Dear Sis,

A miracle happened on this 20th of June —
Sally's birthday. For almost a year, I haven't been
able to face the beauties of our old hiking trail.
Dick is here on one of his infrequent visits — his
old room is always ready and waiting for him —
but his presence has not succeeded in lightening
my heavy heart since the loss of my dear Sally.

Then the miracle happened! The houndmaster
at the Kennel Club invited me to go "walking the
hounds". There are fifty foxhounds that are walked
en masse along country roads every day. A kind of
loving understanding exists between the master
and the hounds. He speaks to them in a firm but
gently musical voice. Mr Thomas is his name.

"Come on out now," he said, and the pack of
hounds left the kennel and headed for the road.

"Come this way now." They followed him to the
left.

My job was to bring up the rear and coax
stragglers back to the group. Both Mr Thomas and
I had whips — but only to crack the ground and
get their attention.

There was hardly any traffic on that back road,
but when a vehicle appeared, Mr Thomas would
say, "Come over here now," and they would herd
to the right or left. They could read his mind, I was
sure. Once, a farmer stopped his truck and said,
"Purtiest thing I ever seen!"

And I was part of it. The countryside was
beautiful. The air was fresh and uplifting. I walked

with a springy step as the emotional burden of the past year began to disappear.

By the time I returned to the club, and Mr Thomas had said, "Kennel up now" . . . I wanted to go walking the gorge once more! All the wonders of nature that I enjoyed with my dear Sally came rushing back with love instead of sorrow.

Dick is spending a couple of weeks here, and I even invited him to go along on Sunday. To my delight he agreed and said he would go into town for some hiking shoes.

Dear Sis — Be glad for me. I feel as if an angel dipped a wing over my troubled brow.

With love from Bud

P.S. Why don't you come for a visit? It's been so long! Exchanging snapshots isn't "where it's at" — to quote Dickie Bird. Don't worry, Sis. I won't make you go hiking.

Slowly and thoughtfully Qwilleran placed the photocopied letter back in the box. There was a tingling in the roots of his moustache that disturbed him.

He looked at his watch; it was not too late to phone his friend Kip MacDiarmid, editor of the *Lockmaster Ledger*.

"Qwill! Speak of the devil — We were talking about you at the Lit Club last night. They want to know when you're coming down to our meeting again."

"As a guest? Or do I have to pay for my own dinner?"

"Put it on your expense account," said the editor.

After the usual amount of banter Qwilleran said, "I'll be in Lockmaster Monday. Would you be free for lunch? I want to discuss a book I'm thinking of writing, and it would help if you could copy some news clips for me."

Arrangements were made.

By long experience Qwilleran knew that newspapermen always know the story-behind-the-story, and it was more often true than false. He also had a ploy for uncovering buried facts and/or rumors. "I'm writing a book," he would say. Laymen and professionals were always willing — even eager — to talk to the purported author of a book that would never be written.

CHAPTER
NINETEEN

On Saturday morning Qwilleran drove down-town to buy a flowering plant to celebrate Polly's return from Chicago. He parked in the municipal lot and was walking toward the Main Street stores when the friendly toot-toot of a horn attracted his attention. Fran Brodie lowered her car window and beckoned. "Have you heard the news?" she asked.

"Is it going to rain?" he asked, although he could tell by her expression that the news was not good.

"I think I'm losing my assistant — after all the time and training I invested in her. I even took her to California on the Thackeray job."

"What's her reason?" Qwilleran asked.

"She's getting married and may move out of town, where her fiancé is investigating a new job."

That would be the Holmes girl and her Dr Watson, Qwilleran thought, and it was a legitimate reason, but Fran wanted only sympathy, so he consoled her.

"Amanda will have to spend more time in the studio and less at City Hall."

"You try telling her that!" Fran replied sourly.

Qwilleran, instead of buying potted tulips, went to Amanda's studio. Lucinda was sitting at the consultation desk, and a young man lounged casually in one of the chairs for clients. But the radiant expression on both faces was not that of a designer-client relationship.

"Hi, Lucinda," Quilleran said. "I thought I would browse for a few minutes before picking Polly up at the airport."

"Hi, Mr Q!" she said, waving a hand with a sparkler on the third finger. "This is Blake Watson."

"Hi, Mr Q," he said, jumping to his feet.

Qwilleran said, "If that ring means what I think it means, best wishes to you both. What are your plans?"

Lucinda said proudly, "We'll be married in June, and then move to Minneapolis, if Blake takes the position that's been offered him."

Blake said, "They're impressed by my five years with Dr Thurston. That's how well known he was in the profession. But when he died and the clinic changed hands, they started cutting corners."

"That often happens," Qwilleran murmured. "Lucky they didn't buy the Thackeray name."

"Sure is! . . . but you have to meet a plane, and I'm keeping you."

When Qwilleran drove Polly home from the airport Saturday noon, he asked if she would like to stop for a little lunch at Onoosh's.

"Thanks, but I'd rather go home and collapse and see my Brutus and Catta."

"I stopped in twice during the week, and they seemed to be in good spirits and amply fed. Your cat-sitter left a report on the kitchen table each morning and filled the automatic feeder for their dinner."

"Yes, she's very conscientious and absolutely trustworthy. She goes to my church." Polly glanced at the landscape. "Everything looks dry. We need rain."

"Were there any momentous decisions made about the bookstore?"

"Yes and no, but it's all strictly confidential. They don't want it known until the plans are final, and I don't want it known that I'm leaving the library at the end of the year."

"Then tell me while we're driving," he said. "There are no spies in the backseat. I checked."

Polly was too tired to appreciate the whimsy of his remarks.

"Well, they've definitely decided to build on the site of Eddington's old store. And the realty experts who visited Pickax said that Book Alley is really an alley, and the old store faced the back of the post office with its trucks and loading dock. So the new building should have its entrance on Walnut Street. I didn't tell them about the buried treasure. I didn't want to lose my credibility. You can tell them about that later on."

As Qwilleran understood it, Eddington's grandfather was a blacksmith who moonlighted as a pirate and buried his loot under a tree in the backyard. After he died — or failed to come home — his wife discovered his secret and had the yard paved with cobblestones. She told the story to Eddington on her deathbed. Whether or not he believed it, he covered the cobblestones with asphalt and it would be one of the legends reported in Qwilleran's collection of *Short & Tall Tales*.

Qwilleran said, "The thought of the Klingenschoen Foundation digging for pirate's treasure under the parking lot before building the bookstore strikes me as highly amusing. The question is: Whether it is better to dig and be disappointed — or not dig and be forever unsure."

They rode in silence for a while, considering the options.

"I admit I had stage fright about brainstorming with the Klingenschoen think tank, but they were all relaxed and jolly, and it was fun."

"There were suggestions like . . . No food, no gifts, no greeting cards . . . A special-events room for book reviews, signings, and literary discussions, with guest speakers . . . Sponsorship of a Literary Club . . . Donation of a percentage of each sale to the Literacy Council . . . No videos . . . A room for large-print and recorded books . . . One wing of the store for preowned books, to be named the Eddington Smith Room . . . Children's programs without lollipops . . . Purchase of the vacant lots across from the entrance — to turn into a grassy park."

"Did you broach your pet idea?" Qwilleran asked.

"Yes, I told them that in the nineteenth century, the stores on Main Street had living quarters on the second floor, and it was considered smart for a merchant to live over the store. That changed with the coming of the automobile and suburban living, and the upstairs rooms are now used for storage and offices. Today we have a shortage of downtown apartments for singles and young marrieds. Also, there are professionals living around the county who would appreciate a pied-à-terre downtown. And there are MCCC faculty members who come up here to teach two or three days a week and would prefer a studio apartment to a hotel room. And the idea of an apartment *over a bookstore* with a view of a grassy park would appeal to intellectuals . . . Well, Qwill, imagine my surprise when they applauded!"

"No wonder, Polly. It was good reasoning, and it came from a good-looking woman with a mesmerizing voice!"

She demurred modestly, and for a while they drove in the preoccupied silence that can be enjoyed by two close friends.

"What did you bring me from Chicago?" he asked.

"A Prokofiev opera on CD. I'm dying to hear it on the barn stereo."

"We'll play it tomorrow — after brunch at Tipsy's."

"It's in Russian, of course, based on a novel by Dostoevsky — all about scandal, intrigue, falsity, and greed."

"Sounds just like Pickax," he said.

Tipsy's Tavern was a roadhouse in a sprawling log cabin — with a yardful of hens and a menu of two dozen interesting egg dishes. Qwilleran ordered ham and eggs with home fries; Polly chose poached eggs on corn pancakes topped with melted cheddar and served with homemade apple chutney. She said it was good but they made the mistake of leaving the raisins whole. "It's

195

important for the raisins to lose their identity," she said.

After that, they went to the barn to listen to the new recording. Qwilleran had only recently become interested in opera, and it was chiefly to please Polly and show off the barn's magnificent acoustics. The Siamese always joined the audience — more for togetherness than appreciation of music. The first soprano aria always had them covering their ears with their hind legs.

Before the music started, Qwilleran served glasses of pineapple juice on a Shaker-style wood tray.

"Where's your silver tray?" Polly asked.

"I haven't been able to find it since cleaning day. I left it out for Mrs Fulgrove to polish, and she has a habit of putting things away where they don't belong. I haven't had time to do a thorough search as yet."

Polly said, "I was unable to find a libretto in English. I have the scenario, though. It's in four acts."

The action took place in the gambling casino of a spa, where men and women won and lost fortunes, borrowed money to pay debts, trusted no one, lied to support their addiction. An aged woman gambled away the fortune that her heirs were waiting to inherit.

Koko hated it! The first act had barely begun, when he raised an indignant howl and continued to scold the speakers until he was banished to the gazebo.

"He doesn't like Prokofiev," Qwilleran explained. But he wondered, How could that cat sense the theme of an opera titled *The Gambler*?

★　★　★

Monday morning Qwilleran drove to Lockmaster to meet Kip MacDiarmid at Inglehart House, a restaurant operated by Bushy's ex-wife. Inglehart was a famous name in that town, and this was a historic mansion on the main thoroughfare. The conversation started in a predictable manner.

Qwilleran said, "How's Moira? . . . Are you taking any trips? . . . Did you decide to get a new puppy? . . . What's new at the Lit Club? . . . We need rain, don't we?"

Kip said, "The Lit Club enjoyed *Cool Koko's Almanac* . . . How's Bushy doing? I see his credit line. Moira wants me to ask if he ever remarried . . . Are you taking any trips? . . . How's Polly? . . . Now what's this book you have in mind?"

Qwilleran said, "A bio of the Thackeray twins, born in Moose County about eight decades ago. Thelma has just returned after a successful career in California; you know about Thurston's animal clinic."

"It was ahead of its time," Kip explained. "Moira used to take our pets there, and she said Dr Thurston was something special — not only his skills but also his caring attitude. The Thackeray Estate sold it to a consortium, and it's now the Whinny Hills Animal Clinic."

"What I can't find out is the cause of Dr Thurston's death. That's why I'm here."

"I've brought you copies of all the clips in the file. The rumormongers had a field day. They considered it suicide because he was depressed after the death of his wife. But it was officially ruled an accident. A recent rain — slippery rocks on the edge of the gorge — perhaps a momentary dizzy spell. He was getting on in years."

"Who were his heirs?" Qwilleran asked.

"He left his house to the county for a horse museum, his liquid assets to his sister, and the clinic to his son, Dick."

"What's Dick's line of work?"

"Good question. He's always pursued his business interests in other parts of the country, coming home to visit his parents at intervals . . . I might add that he was involved in a fracas a couple of years ago when he applied for a permit to operate a motorbike dirt-racing track. He had acquired some acreage in the western part of the county, near some posh condos. The neighbors rose up in arms. They virtually rioted at a meeting of the county commissioners. They bombarded the *Ledger* with angry letters to the editor, opposing the proposed venture on grounds of noise, dust, weekend traffic on quiet country roads, disturbance of the Sabbath peace, and lessening of property values."

Qwilleran shook his head sympathetically. "This must have been painful to Dr Thurston."

"His clients and admirers considered it an outrage, and the scuttlebutt was that Dick acquired the acreage as payment of a gambling debt owed him. The doctor had never accepted the notion that Dick was a compulsive gambler, but — sub rosa — it was considered a fact."

Quilleran felt a tingling in the roots of his moustache as he recalled Koko's tantrum during the Russian opera. "What was the outcome?"

"Dick disappeared from the local scene, and the acreage was put up for sale. The consensus was that his father paid him to leave town. It must have been a crushing blow, so soon after the death of Dr Sally."

"Dick's former schoolmates said he used to be very popular. Too bad he turned out to be a blot on the Thackeray escutcheon," Qwilleran said.

"Yes, he made a few enemies in Lockmaster during the motorbike episode." The editor lowered his voice. "In fact, when the suicide rumor was ruled out, there were quite a few hints of patricide. Dick was so quick to sell his father's clinic that the accident on the gorge trail began to look fishy to many locals."

"Dick told the police that his father went out at day-break as a matter of course — to avoid the crowds of Sunday hikers. He said he would be home by noon and they would go out for Sunday brunch at the Palomino Paddock. When the doc didn't return by three o'clock, Dick notified the police . . . It's all in these clippings I've brought you. The amateur sleuths even brought up the question of hiking shoes. Dick claimed he never went hiking; a local store claimed that he bought a pair of hiking shoes the day before his dad's accident . . . It would have been ludicrous if it weren't so tragic."

On Monday evening, the shuttle flight bounced to a stop, and the passengers emerged, carrying briefcases or shopping bags. A husky gray-haired man carrying a duffel bag came down the ramp with quick glances to right and left.

Qwilleran stepped forward. "Mr Simmons? Qwilleran's Limousine Service."

The duffel bag was transferred to the other hand and the right hand shot out. "You're the famous Qwill! I'm Mark Simmons."

"Welcome to Moose County! Do you have other luggage?"

"One bag. Thelma told me to bring my tux."

"What does the bag look like?"

"Blue nylon. Red stripe."

"Hi, Mr Q!" the baggage handler said. "Which one is yours?"

"Blue nylon. Red stripe. But I'll take anything that looks good."

The visitor was filling his lungs. "The air smells good. What do you do to it?"

"Secret formula. Don't breathe too deeply or you'll float away."

As soon as they were in the SUV and headed for Pickax, the conversation started and never stopped.

"How d'you like our Thelma, Qwill?"

"She's a grand lady! But she's not yours! She's ours, and we let California have her for sixty years. You're not a native of the West Coast?"

"Sure ain't! I'm a Hoosier. Met a girl from L.A. when I was in the armed services and followed her out there. Perfect marriage. Two sons, one daughter — all married. Grandkids on the way. Can't complain. Had my good years. Widowed six years ago. Retired for five. Do a few security jobs. That's how I met Thelma."

"I understand you've been a great help to her, Mark."

"Call me Simmons. That's what I was in the Army and that's what I was on the police force. Only Thelma adds the Mister."

"Thelma and *The New York Times*," Qwilleran muttered.

"Thelma's a smart woman, but I don't see why — at her time of life — she should come here to help her nephew, a grown man . . . You've met him, Qwill. What do you think of him?"

"He smiles a lot."

"Sure does! . . . What's that thing over there?" He pointed to a tall, weatherbeaten shack.

"A shaft house. It marks the site of an abandoned mine. There were ten mines here. When they closed, Moose County went into a three-decade depression."

"Thelma told me about it. Her dad — she calls him Pop — was a poor potato farmer until he got into the potato chip business."

Qwilleran glanced at his passenger, looking for a glimmer of tongue-in-cheek or twinkle-in-eye. There was none. The potato chip myth had reached the West Coast.

Qwilleran asked, "Did Thelma tell you about my barn?"

"Sure did. I'm looking forward to seeing it."

"Then I have a suggestion," Qwilleran said. "Since Thelma's spare room is occupied by her nephew while the Film Club is getting under way, she planned to put you up at a hotel, but there's a vacant apartment near my barn that you may as well use. It's only a few blocks from Pleasant Street, and she'll give you the keys to one of her vehicles, so you can come and go as you please."

"Sounds good," Simmons said. "Better than being holed up with two females, five parrots, and a guy who smiles all the time. Much as I like Janice's cooking, I have to say that I've eaten enough of her waffles to sink a battleship. Have you met Janice?"

"Oh, yes. She's a nice young woman — very thoughtful and devoted to Thelma. She said she would come to the apartment and make up the bed, hang towels, and leave a little something in the refrigerator for you."

"That sounds like Janice," Simmons said.

At a certain point on Main Street Qwilleran pulled to the curb. "Look down that street. What does it look like?"

"Disneyland."

"That's Pleasant Street, and Thelma has the third house on the left."

At a traffic circle, Qwilleran turned into the driveway of a large fieldstone building. "That once a mansion filled with antiques, but it was gutted by fire . . . Arson, you'll be interested to know . . . Now it's a small theatre for live productions . . . The former carriage house at the rear had stalls for four carriages and servants' quarters upstairs. That's where you're going to bunk while you're here . . . I suggest we drop your luggage there and then drive through the woods to my barn and have a drink."

"I may never return to California," the guest said.

"How do you feel about cats? I have two Siamese."

"Cats, dogs, hamsters, white mice! My kids had 'em all. Thelma hates cats!"

"I know. They were kept out of sight during the champagne reception here."

They drove through the dense woods and emerged in a clearing, where the four-story octagonal barn loomed like a medieval castle.

"I don't believe it!" Simmons said.

"Wait till you see the interior!"

Qwilleran was accustomed to the gasps, gulps, and speechlessness of first-time visitors, but this Hoosier from Hollywood seemed stunned by the vast spaces, the balconies and ramps, the rafters four stories overhead, the large white cube in the middle of it all.

"How about a drink?" Qwilleran asked.

The guest came out of his trance long enough to say, "A little bourbon and water."

CHAPTER
TWENTY

Thelma's Mr Simmons was enjoying the barn so much — and the attentions of the Siamese — that he was reluctant to leave when Janice came to pick him up. They were going to dinner at the Grist Mill and Qwilleran was invited. He declined, saying he had to attend a very important meeting.

It was the dress rehearsal for the Kit Kat Revue, and it proved Qwilleran's contention that a cat trained to walk on a leash will walk where he wants to walk and not where he's told to walk. Wetherby's Jet Stream acted as if he had fleas and sat down center-stage to scratch. Nick Bamba's Nicodemus kept sniffing invisible spots on the floor and baring his fangs in an expression of disgust. It was decided that all cats would be carried or otherwise conveyed. Apart from that, all went well. The creative dance club from the high school and the tumbling team rehearsed to get the feel of the stage — and the feel of their furry costumes with tails.

Bushy was there to project his slides of kittens on the backdrop. The idea was to show a different slide for each act. He had photographed them in all the kitten colonies on Pleasant Street: tiny creatures with large ears and floppy feet and comical markings. There was a mother cat suckling her brood, playing games with her soft paw, fondly carrying them around by the scruff of the neck.

Then there was a run-through of the grand finale. All cats had been brought to the opera house in carriers, and they would remain cooped up until it was time for them to go on — sequestered in the various dressing rooms and offices backstage. It was hoped that this would prevent squabbles.

Hixie said to the prominent citizens who awaited briefing, "Until the finale, it will have been a program of lighthearted song and dance and humorous verse. Suddenly the mood changes. A recording of Elgar's 'Pomp and Circumstance' fills the hall, signifying a solemn occasion, and the procession of prominent citizens begins — one by one — walking with dignity — carrying a beloved pet."

Qwilleran said, "Suppose there are whistles and shouts from the audience?"

"They'll be instructed to limit responses to polite applause," Hixie said. "When the last cat is off the stage, there will be whistles and shouts and a standing ovation."

"What should we wear?" someone asked.

"Anything of neutral color — gray, tan, brown, black — whatever will show off your cat's coloring."

"What about the harmless herbal sedative?"

"We have an envelope for each of you, containing a capsule that is to be broken open and the powder sprinkled on the cat's meal beforehand."

Someone said, "Do you have any extras? I could use one myself!"

The following evening, supporters of the Kit Kat Agenda would have a preview of the renovated opera house, twenty-four hours before Thelma's gala first night. It was a memory to boast about in years to come — for more reasons than one.

The red carpet was on the sidewalk. There was a canvas marquee at the entrance. A cordon of press photographers waited. And a flock of MCCC students in KIT KAT T-shirts would park cars, earning credits for community service.

It was a black-tie event, and patrons arrived in dinner jackets and long dresses, to be seated in comfortable swivel chairs at round cabaret tables. Then more students in KIT KAT T-shirts served chilled splits of champagne and hollow-stemmed plastic wine glasses.

When the lights dimmed, the master of ceremonies, Wetherby Goode, welcomed them in his irreverent style, then sat down at the piano and played "Kitten on the Keys." It was a finger-tickling number that had been played by Moose County piano students for seventy-five years. Wetherby played it faster.

Then Hannah MacLeod sang Noel Coward's "Chase Me, Charlie, Over the Garden Wall". Qwilleran read T. S. Eliot's whimsical verses about jellicle cats and such famous felines as Skimbleshanks and Bustopher Jones. The cat dancers danced and the cat tumblers tumbled. In between, the six-foot-eight Derek Cuttlebrink, Moose County's gift to country western, loped into the spotlight, strummed his guitar, and sang original lyrics, such as:

> Kit Kat kittens have love to give,
> Kit Kat kittens are fun!
> A handful of fur, just learning to purr —
> Two are better than one.

All the while, the audience was enchanted by the changing background of kittenlife.

Then the stage blacked out for a moment, and the sonorous chords of "Pomp and Circumstance" filled the hall and a disembodied voice said, "During the following presentation of cats marching to save kittens, please limit your response to polite applause."

The solemn procession began. Each pair was announced by the "voice." Each pair moved slowly across the stage without acknowledging the polite applause.

"Her Honor, Mayor Amanda Goodwinter . . . and Quincy."

"The WPKX meteorologist, Wetherby Goode . . . and Jet Stream."

"Food editor for the *Moose County Something*, Mildred Riker . . . and Toulouse."

"Prize-winning woodcrafter Douglas Bethune . . . and Winston Churchill."

"Dr Diane Lanspeak . . . and Hypo."

"Nutcracker Innkeeper, Nick Bamba . . . and Nicodemus."

"Professors Jennie and Ruth Cavendish . . . with Pinky and Quinky, short for Propinquity and Equanimity."

"High-school custodian for forty years, Pat O'Dell . . . with Wrigley."

"Superintendent of schools, Lyle Compton . . . and Socrates."

"Director of the public library, Polly Duncan . . . and Brutus."

"And last but not least, columnist James Mackintosh Qwilleran . . . and Kao K'o Kung."

The polite applause reached a crescendo. Murmurs of enjoyment became a roar of approval. Someone shouted, "Cool Koko."

The cat riding on Qwilleran's shoulder stared with alarm at the darkened hall. Then, blinded by stage lights, he sprang into the air, wrenching the leash from Qwilleran's grasp. He flew off the stage into the first row of tables. The shouts and screams only alarmed him more, and he went flying around the hall with leash trailing — jumping over heads, landing on backs and shoulders, while champagne bottles and glasses scattered.

"Close the doors!" Qwilleran yelled. Thwarted in his escape, Koko turned and scampered across more tables and patrons, until something stopped him abruptly.

"TREAT!" Qwilleran thundered, and the cat returned to the stage, pouncing on a few more heads and a few more shoulders.

By the time Qwilleran had grabbed the frantic animal, the other cats had gone home, and their rhinestone harnesses were on a table backstage. Koko's was added to the pile, and he was stuffed into his carrier — to wait while Qwilleran helped the others clean up.

Hixie, the MacLeods, and Mavis Adams were picking up empty bottles and plastic glasses. Fortunately, nothing had spilled or broken. Cabaret tables and chairs had simply to be restored to their orderly rows.

Hixie said, "That Koko really knows how to bring down the house!"

Qwilleran grunted with irritation. "His performance won't do any good for the adopt-a-kitten campaign."

"Did you give him the sedative?"

"I sprinkled it on his food, as you instructed."

Then he had a sudden hollow feeling. He tossed the carrier in the backseat and drove to the barn in a hurry. Leaving Koko in the car, he rushed indoors to look at the cats' plates under the kitchen table.

Both plates were licked clean. Had Koko eaten the wrong one? Where was Yum Yum? He found her on the hearth rug, lying flat-out on her side. He spoke her name, and she raised her head and gave him a glassy stare . . . It was all evident. Koko had sensed that something unacceptable had been added to his dish. He pushed Yum Yum aside and ate the contents of her plate and she consumed the harmless herbal sedative. She liked it!

In a few minutes Polly phoned from Indian Village.

"Qwill! What happened? Wasn't Koko sedated?"

"You won't believe this!" he said. "The cats never change plates. Koko's is always on the right, and he knows right from left, but he detected a foreign substance. Somehow he convinced Yum Yum to change plates. She not only got the sedative but a larger serving of food than usual. She's bushed!!"

The first week of the Film Club would also become noted for the "electrical storm of the century" in Moose County. According to the meteorologist, a weather front was stalled over Canada, gathering fury by the day. Bushy postponed the cruise for Thelma, Janice, and their guest; Qwilleran filed his copy early and returned to the snug safety of the barn; the Siamese were nervous.

Then there was a phone call from Simmons.

"Are you busy, Qwill? Thelma wants me to deliver something." A few minutes later the green coupé pulled into the barnyard.

"Are you comfortable in the carriage house apartment?" Qwilleran asked.

"Very! I'll hate to leave."

"Don't be in a hurry," Qwilleran said. "It's vacant for the month of May. Be my guest . . . How about a little bourbon and water?"

"Won't hurt. And may help." He handed over a plastic shopping bag.

Peering into it, Qwilleran said, "I don't believe this. Where did she find it?"

"It's a long story," his guest said.

After they settled into the deep-cushioned sofas, there was the usual talk about the weather. The big electrical storm was on the way. Koko's fur was

210

standing on end as if electrified. He kept washing over his ear — with his left paw, not his right. Then he would tear up the ramp at ninety miles an hour — then race back down again. Yum Yum had already burrowed under the hearth rug.

"Let's hear the long story," Qwilleran suggested casually.

"Well!" said his guest. "Thelma went to the club in early morning, when Dick was not there — to see if everything was being done right. He had furnished his private office lavishly, she thought. Included was a small bar with several bottles of liquor. There were also two cut-glass decanters. She wondered if they were Waterford. There was a silver tray. She wondered if it was sterling. Turning it over, she found your name inscribed . . . She decided not to mention it to Dick. She would just take it. And here it is!"

Qwilleran thought, It figures! . . . The cleaning crew was here . . . I was helping Bushy shoot hats . . . Dick delivered a gift . . . he saw the tray Mrs Fulgrove had polished . . .

"Well! Thank you! What else can I say?"

Simmons said, "You can agree with me that the guy's a kleptomaniac! Thelma's finally getting that idea. In fact, she went through Dick's desk, looking for a valuable object that disappeared from her house, but all she found was a handgun in the bottom drawer. She wondered if it was registered."

"All very interesting, Simmons. What was the valuable object?"

"A wristwatch of Pop's that she'd had on her dressing table for forty years! It was a gold Rolex with winding stem."

"May I refresh your drink?"

Simmons sipped in thoughtful silence for a while, as Yum Yum played with his shoelace. Then he said suddenly, "Do you use a pocket tape recorder, Qwill?"

"All the time."

"I've brought one for Thelma. A woman of her age and wealth and position should have one on her person at all times. She's had a couple of run-ins with Smiley and who knows what that four-flusher has up his sleeve. To tell the truth, Qwill, I'm worried about Thelma . . . She seems to think she put him in his place, but can he be trusted? He shows all the symptoms of a compulsive gambler. He could turn to crime to pay off gambling debts — or get wiped out if he defaults. Thelma won't accept the fact that he's a gambler, any more than she'll admit that her pop was a bootlegger. Why? Is it because she's so protective of her image?"

"You knew about the bootlegging?" Qwilleran asked.

"I know that this coastline was a major port of entry for contraband from Canada, which is more than you can say for potato chips."

Qwilleran said, "Denial seems to run in the family. I've read all her brother's letters, and he mentions Dick's financial troubles but never his gambling, although it's considered a fact among those who claim to know."

"Ever since his father died, Smiley has been coming to California and buttering up his aunt."

"Yow!" Koko howled with piercing intensity, and at the same moment blue-white lightning flashed in the many odd-shaped windows of the barn, followed immediately by the crack and rumble of thunder that reverberated in the vast interior. The wind howled. The rain lashed the walls of the barn.

Conversation was drowned out by the tumult overhead, and the visitor grasped an arm of the sofa and waited for the roof to cave in overhead.

Gradually the intervals between lightning flashes and thunderclaps widened, as the storm moved on to another target, and Qwilleran said, "You have your mud slides and earthquakes. We have our northern hurricanes, and if you liked this, just wait and see what we do with snow!"

The day after the storm, Wetherby Goode said to his listeners on WPKX: "It was fun while it lasted, wasn't it, folks? There's some flooding caused by overloaded storm sewers, but it was the good drenching rain that we hoped for. Now you can take a shower and water the geraniums without feeling guilty, and the weather will smile on the gala opening of Thelma's Film Club. All the first-nighters will be dressed up, and I'll be wearing my new cuff links . . ."

CHAPTER
TWENTY-ONE

On the opening night, Qwilleran and Polly were among those absent. He had explained to Thelma that it was more important to sell their seats to enthusiastic first-nighters. She understood.

Actually they were more interested in the following week's offering — the 1922 talkie release of Eugene O'Neill's prize-winning drama, *Anna Christie*. It was the film in which Garbo's throaty voice was heard on the silver screen for the first time, saying, *Give me viskey, baby, and don't be stingy*.

Qwilleran observed opening-night amenities, however, by sending Thelma a long telegram to the theatre and a dozen red roses to her home.

He and Polly dined at the Grist Mill — at a second seating following one for early show-goers. Derek Cuttlebrink seated them at the table beneath the scythe. He said, "The lobster curry's good tonight."

Qwilleran said, "Does that mean it's usually bad? Or did you sell too little at the first seating — and you're stuck with it?"

Derek smirked and said, "For that remark you get a fly in your soup."

Polly said, "I hope the boss doesn't overhear this exchange of pleasantries."

Elizabeth Hart, the owner, was heading for their table. "Polly, so good to see you! I know you love curry. Try the Lobster Calcutta! . . . Qwill, thank you for sending Thelma to us! She's delivering the hats Sunday, because she's involved with her Film Club till then. We'll open the exhibit the following Saturday. A whole fleet of yachts will be coming over from Grand Island. The media will love it. And we're having a New York model here to model the hats and pose for photographs!"

Both Qwilleran and Polly ordered Lobster Calcutta and enjoyed it. Then he told her about finding the silver tray.

"Where was it?" she asked with concern.

"In a plastic shopping bag."

"That's a good idea. Mrs Fulgrove knows what she's doing. It will keep the tray from tarnishing so fast. Every time you use metal polish on your tray, you know, it loses a minuscule bit of the silver surface."

Then he told her about his pleasant visit with Thelma's Mr Simmons — but not what they talked about. He said, "His first name is Mark."

"I'm very fond of that name," she said. "My father used to say that anyone named Matthew, Mark, Luke, or John has a built-in advantage over the Georges and Walters. His name was Orville."

Qwilleran said, "I've often thought I should write a column on the naming of offspring: Why parents give them the names they do . . . how many persons go through life with a name they don't like. My mother named me Merlin! One man I know narrowly escaped being named Melrose. And how about the fashions in names that change from generation to generation. No girl babies are named Thelma in the twenty-first century. Yet there was once a vogue for female names with 'th' in the spelling: Martha, Bertha, Dorothy, Edith, Faith, Ethel, Samantha, Judith . . ."

Polly said, "Sometimes, Qwill, you sound exactly like my father!"

The next day was a workday for Polly, and so Qwilleran took her home directly after dinner. By the time he arrived at the barn, Koko was doing his grasshopper routine, meaning a message was on the answering machine.

It was from Janice. "Qwill, I need to talk to you. Important. Call me anytime before midnight."

He phoned her immediately. "Is something wrong, Janice?"

"Very sad!" she said in a sorrowful voice. "A message came for Mr Simmons while he was at the club. His daughter in California was in a car crash and is hospitalized in critical condition. He's flying home tomorrow."

"What a shame!" Qwilleran said. "Shall I drive him to the airport?"

"That would help. I'd drive him, but I have to be available for Thelma. There are problems at the club, you know, during its first week. So it's very kind of you, Qwill."

"Not at all. It's the least I can do."

This would be his last chance to talk with Thelma's confidant, adviser, and self-appointed watchdog.

Early Thursday morning Qwilleran picked up the troubled father and asked, "Any news from the hospital?"

"I can't get any information. What happened? Where did it happen? Whose fault was it? She's always been a careful driver. What's the nature of her injuries? I didn't sleep a wink last night. I have a thirty-two-year-old daughter with two kids — who is hospitalized two thousand miles away. I can't worry about an eighty-two-year-old woman with all the money in the world, who's going to leave it to a relative who's a nogoodnik."

"Forget about Thelma," Qwilleran said. "I'll step in and do what needs to be done. But I'll need information from you."

"For one thing, she's given me power of attorney in California, and I told her to name a local person. But so far nothing has been done. When she came here, full of family feeling and generosity, she made a new will, leaving everything to Smiley! A big mistake! It should be changed before it's too late. She admires you, and you could talk some sense into her head! She's a smart, successful, independent, opinionated woman, but she has this simpering sentimentality about her 'dear Bud' who played the flute and loved animals and was so good to his son, giving him everything he wanted . . . and her 'dear Pop' who invented a new kind of potato chip and was so good to his children. He left her his gold Rolex wristwatch, and she kept it wound for forty years. It has always been on her dressing table. It disappeared recently. Go figure."

"One question, Simmons. Did you hear about the kidnapping of the parrots shortly after Thelma arrived?"

"No!" was the thundering reply. "Why didn't she tell me?"

"She was afraid — or embarrassed. I wormed it out of her assistant. It happened on the Sunday of the big welcoming party. Two days before, she had been pictured with two parrots on the front page of the *Something*. But I say that had nothing to do with it. I say it was an inside job. Someone knew about her intense fondness for those birds. Someone knew the family would be out of the house — in fact, all of Pleasant Street was attending the party . . . with one exception. The O'Dells left early, and they saw a delivery van drive around behind the Thackeray house and leave a few minutes later.

"Someone knew that large, talkative birds require caging and covering. Someone knew about Thelma's fabulous jewelry collection, hidden on the premises. The ransom demand specified an instant payoff — or else! Dick made himself a hero by making the transaction and bringing the parrots back alive."

"And the girls didn't suspect him?"

"If they did, Thelma chose to forget it . . . but there's more to the story. On that same night, two vans met on a country road in Bixby County, and large square containers were transferred from one to the other. The sheriff decided they must have been TV sets stolen in a recent burglary at a television store. Before leaving, the driver of the loaded van shot and killed the other. I maintain that the shooter was Dick, and he drove off with the ransom as well as the birds. No doubt he knows a fence who handles stolen jewelry."

Simmons said, "Someone's got to warn that woman!"

"It would be more logical for a longtime friend and security aide to break the news," Qwilleran said. "If you agree, I'll give you some more ammunition . . . When Bud Thackeray fell to his death in the Black Creek Gorge, it was ruled officially to be an accident. But there was a discrepancy between what Dick told the police and what Bud wrote in his last letter to Thelma. Dick, visiting his father, agreed to go hiking with him and would even buy some hiking boots. Yet, the newspaper clippings have Dick waiting for his father to come home from hiking, so they could go out to lunch."

"If I wanted to be a devil's advocate, Qwill, I could say that the reluctant hiker changed his mind. But, from what I know of this particular devil, he has mud on his boots."

Two days after Simmons's sudden departure, three days after the opening of the Film Club, and four days after the great electrical storm, Bushy phoned Qwilleran's barn. "I'm in your neighborhood. Want to hear the latest installment in the Bushland-Thackeray story?"

Qwilleran knew the photographer had sent Thelma glossy prints of her and the parrots.

He knew Bushy had further ingratiated himself by making a print of her brother's portrait — on matte paper suitable for framing.

He knew she had sat for her own portrait in Bushy's studio, after which she said, "It's the best likeness I've ever had. He captured the way I *feel*!"

Now what?

When Bushy arrived, they went to the gazebo with a thermal coffeepot and a plate of shortbread from the Scottish Bakery.

Bushy said, "There's nothing wrong with shortbread that couldn't be improved with chocolate frosting and chopped walnuts."

"They'll never let you into Scotland again, mon! Are you still wowing the potato chip heiress, Bushy?"

"Well, she told me she thinks balding men are sexy. I call her Lady Thelma, and she calls me Mr Bushy. And yesterday she asked me to do a strange favor. She gave me a green card to the late-night show at the Film Club and asked me to do a little spying. That's my word for it. She wanted to know what kind of people attend and how they behave. She said everyone at the early show is appreciative and well mannered."

"Did you go?"

"I told her I'd be tied up until next week but I'd go Wednesday. She told me not to talk to anyone at the club . . . What d'you think, Qwill? Doesn't it sound like she suspects some kind of monkey business at the late show?"

"I believe the apartment dwellers across the street have complained about noise and rowdyism at three in the morning. I'll be curious to know what you find out . . . By the way, has she seen the prints of the hat shots?"

"Yeah, and she flipped over them!"

"Her nephew and Janice are transporting the hats up to Mooseville tomorrow, and I'm driving Thelma. So maybe I'll have something to report."

The twenty-four hat boxes were wedged tightly into Thelma's van on Sunday afternoon. Thelma was as excited as a fond parent seeing her child play the lead in a high-school production of *My Fair Lady*. They took off with the van in the lead; Janice had driven up there before and knew the route. Once they were on Sandpit Road, it was straight going to Mooseville.

In an attempt to calm Thelma's nerves, Qwilleran tried to entertain her with legends of Mooseville: the Sand Giant who lives in the dune overlooking the town and can be heard to grumble when angered . . . and the mysterious fate of the *Jenny Lee*, a fishing boat owned by Bushy's ancestors . . . and —

"Why are those ditches filled with water?" she asked.

"Those are drainage ditches that keep the farmers' fields from being flooded after a heavy rain. You'll notice a lot of farm equipment on this road."

A large tractor was lumbering ahead of them at twenty miles an hour.

"You learn to be patient when you drive through farming country, and you don't complain about mud on the road. This tractor won't be with us long; it's just transferring from one field to another."

It was a two-lane country road, paved but muddy from the treads of farm equipment.

Qwilleran was following the Thackeray van, in front of which was the slow tractor.

Dick Thackeray, driving the van, was not patient. Several times he pulled into the southbound lane in an attempt to pass the slow-moving vehicle, but there was always a southbound vehicle that forced him back in line.

Qwilleran stopped talking and watched the maneuvering with apprehension. "Don't try it, buddy," he said under his breath. Dick tried it. He pulled out of line and accelerated. The tractor driver, from his high perch, waved him back. There was a pickup coming south. Its driver leaned on his horn. Dick kept on going — faster.

Thelma cried, "*What is that fool doing?*"

At the last minute, realizing he couldn't make it, Dick veered left onto the southbound shoulder. It was muddy. The van slid toward the ditch, then toppled over into the water.

"Oh my God!" Thelma screamed. "My hats! . . . *Janice!*"

All traffic had stopped. Thelma was fumbling with her safety belt."

"No! Stay here!" Qwilleran was calling 911 on the cell phone. The truck driver could be seen doing the same. Thelma was fumbling for the door handle, and he

222

grabbed her left forearm so tightly that she cried out in pain.

The farmer had jumped down and was heading for the van, which was upside down and half submerged. The truck driver waved all approaching traffic to the northbound lane — to keep the road open for emergency vehicles. In a minute or two their sirens could be heard; the First Responders . . . a sheriff's patrol . . . the Rescue Squad . . . two ambulances, one from each direction . . . another patrol car . . . a tow truck with a winch.

Qwilleran had released his grip, and Thelma covered her face with her hands and moaned, "That fool! That fool!"

What could he say? How could he comfort her? He had seen the alligator-print boxes float away in the muddy ditch, then sink. He spoke her name, and there was no answer. Fearing she was in shock, he called to a deputy:

"She saw the accident. Family members are in the van. I'm worried. She's in her eighties."

A medic came to check her vital signs.

"She's okay," he reported to Qwilleran. "She's angry that's all. Madder'n a wet hen!"

The accident victims were lifted from the wreck and put on stretchers, to be whisked by ambulance to the Pickax hospital.

Qwilleran said to Thelma, "They both seemed to be conscious. I'll call the hospital after a while. Meanwhile I should make a few phone calls. Excuse me." He stepped out of the car, taking the cell phone and a county phone book from the pocket in the door.

First he called Elizabeth Hart, who was shocked, then concerned about Thelma, then dismayed over the ruined plans.

He notified Thelma's physician, Diane Lanspeak, at home in Indian Village.

He also called Celia O'Dell, who had been a volunteer care-giver and knew exactly what to do and say. She said she would be standing by. She was waiting for them when they returned to Pleasant Street. She asked Thelma if she would like a cup of cocoa.

"All I want is to sit in my Pyramid for a while."

Soon, Dr Diane phoned. She had called the hospital and learned that the two accident victims were being treated and released.

Qwilleran huffed into his moustache. He was not eager to face Thelma's fool nephew and mouth the usual polite claptrap, and he was glad when Celia said her husband would pick them up.

It had not been Qwilleran's idea of a pleasant Sunday afternoon in May.

And it was not over!

When he returned to the barn, the self-appointed monitor of the answering machine was going wild. It was mystifying how that cat could tell the difference between an important message and a nuisance call. Could he sense urgency in the tone of voice?

The first message was from Simmons: "Sorry to miss your call. I've been baby-sitting with the grandkids. My daughter has a fractured pelvis. Painful, but could be worse. As soon as things straighten out, I'll read the riot act to Thelma — tell her what I learned from you about the kidnapping and her brother's so-called accident. She should dump that guy!"

Qwilleran thought, Wait till he hears about the hats!

The message from Bushy was his espionage report. "The late-night film ended at midnight. Half the audience went home. The others went backstage for booze, slot machines and — believe it or not — a porno film on a smaller screen. It was that real sick stuff! How can I tell Thelma about this? She'll have a stroke! I checked vehicle tags in the parking lot. Mostly from Bixby County."

CHAPTER
TWENTY-TWO

As someone who liked publicity, Thelma was getting more than her share. "Thackeray" had become a buzzword among headline writers in Moose County. Her opening of the Film Club and her magnanimous loan of the opera house to an animal-rescue cause put her in the limelight, but not all the news was good.

On Monday the banner headline read: 24 WORKS OF ART DROWNED IN DITCH. Dick Thackeray Cited for Reckless Driving.

On Tuesday the news was better but less dramatic: LOST CHURCH FOUND IN FOREST. Thackerays Buried in Graveyard of Tiny Log Chapel.

There was no name-dropping on Wednesday: PUBLIC REST ROOMS SLATED FOR DOWNTOWN PICKAX. Merchants and Shoppers Applaud Town Council's Decision.

On Thursday morning Bushy stopped at the barn on the way to cover an assignment for the paper. "The newsroom is hot this morning. Thought you'd want to know. It ties in with the bad news I had to report to Thelma. If she didn't have a stroke then, she'll have one when she reads today's headline."

226

Thursday's headline read: INDECENT EXPOSURE LANDS 3 IN JAIL. Members of Film Club Nabbed While Strip-Dancing in Parking Lot.

As soon as papers were delivered to the library, Polly phoned Qwilleran. "That poor woman! My heart bleeds for her! But I can't think of anything we can do."

He was silent.

"Qwill, did you hear what I said?"

"I'm thinking . . . Thelma's a trouper! She'll drink a lot of cocoa and sit in her Pyramid and the club will continue as if nothing had happened."

Later, to confirm his prediction, he phoned the club and heard a recorded message:

"Seats for tonight's showing of *Anna Christie* featuring Garbo are sold out. If you want to make a reservation for future shows, press one. Next week's billing: *City Lights* (1931). Charlie Chaplin's last completely silent film."

It wasn't until Friday, however, that Qwilleran's low blood pressure started to rise. His friends at the *Something* were always eager to tip him off. And in this case they knew he had a special interest in Thelma Thackeray.

First Bushy phoned from his van. "One of the guys in the lab was sent out to get a shot of the entrance of the Film Club. They say it's closed until further notice."

Roger MacGillivray, a longtime friend, phoned Qwilleran on the way to the police station. "There's been a shooting at the club," he said.

And the managing editor phoned and said, "Qwill, how fast can you get your copy in? We've got an early deadline. There's been a murder."

The Friday headline read: MANAGER OF FILM CLUB SHOT DURING BURGLARY. Dick Thackeray's Body Found by Janitors. Safe Cracked.

Qwilleran was taken aback — not because of the murder; after all, Dick moved in questionable circles. What daunted him was Koko's behavior in the middle of the night — not howling . . . more like . . . crowing! It had been the kind of strident, affirmative communication that could now be interpreted as "I told you so!" . . . That cat! At the time, when Qwilleran was wakened so rudely, he thought Koko had swallowed something unacceptable and he would upchuck in some unacceptable place. But now . . . the incident assumed new meaning.

Qwilleran sent Thelma flowers and a note of consolation, resisting the urge to say "Good riddance!" When he phoned Simmons in California, the security man said, "Well, that solves the security problem, doesn't it? Too bad she won't continue it and hire a manager . . . I wouldn't mind handling it myself. I'd enjoy working for her again."

Then there was another call from Bushy. "Well how about it, Qwill? I feel sorry for Thelma. This really messes up her plans, doesn't it? I wish there was something I could do. But I don't want to step out of line."

"How about taking her and Janice for a cruise Sunday afternoon. It's peaceful out on the lake. It might be therapeutic. Call Janice and sound her out. I think she'll agree."

As for the author of the "Qwill Pen," he had never really wanted to write a biography of Bud and Sis. But "The Last of the Thackerays" would make a fascinating legend for *Short & Tall Tales*. He would have to work fast if he wanted to interview her in depth; she was, after all, eighty-two.

He was not fast enough. In Monday's newspaper there was a news bulletin important enough to warrant a remake of the front page. A black-bordered box focused attention on the sad news: "Thelma Thackeray, 82, died peacefully in her sleep early this morning, at her home on Pleasant Street. She recently returned from a sixty-year career in Hollywood, CA, to found Thelma's Film Club. She was the last of the Moose County Thackerays. Obituary on Wednesday."

Qwilleran subdued his urge to phone Janice for details, knowing she would be busy with helpful neighbors. Burgess Campbell, as the Duke of Pleasant Street, would be supervising the arrangements. Mavis Adams was Thelma's attorney. Celia and Pat O'Dell would be enormously helpful.

He was surprised, therefore, when Janice called him. "May I drive over there, Qwill? I need your advice."

Within a few minutes the green coupé pulled into the barnyard, and he went out to meet her. Besides her usual shoulder bag she was carrying one of Thelma's capacious satchel-bags of soft leather. It was bulging as if it contained a watermelon. He refrained from commenting.

"Let's sit in the library," he said.

The old books that covered one wall of the fireplace cube from top to bottom made a comforting atmosphere for confidences.

"So many books!" she said.

"That's only half of them. The rest are in my studio . . . Now, how can I help you, Janice?"

"I don't know whether I did the right thing."

"What did you do?" he asked in a kindly voice, although though he was bristling with curiosity. "Would you like a little fruit juice? A glass of wine?"

"Well . . . yes . . . I think I'd like a glass of wine."

The white Zinfandel relaxed her, but Qwilleran continued to bristle.

"Thelma's always an early riser, and I knocked on her door to see if she'd like a cup of tea. She was still under the covers, but I got a sick feeling when I saw a liquor bottle on the bedside table — the bourbon that we bought for Mr Simmons. Thelma's always had chronic pancreatitis and was supposed to avoid stress and alcohol —"

"She's had plenty of stress lately," Qwilleran interrupted.

"Dr Diane put 'acute pancreatitis' on the death certificate."

They were both silent for a while, Qwilleran remembering how Thelma had said, "I've got to be a very good girl."

Janice was fidgeting and glancing at Thelma's handbag on the desk. "There's something I want to tell you, Qwill . . . about what we did Thursday night. Or Friday morning, really. Thelma said she wanted me to drive her to the club at about two-thirty A.M., and she told me to take a nap and set the alarm clock for two o'clock. When we got there, a few cars were still in the lot, and we parked at the curb until they were all gone except Dick's loaner. He wrecked his old van, you know."

"I well remember!"

"She told me to stay in the car, and when she came out a few minutes later, she was smiling, and her big handbag was stuffed full of something. She said, 'All's well that ends well.' One thing I had learned was not to ask questions. She was quite calm all weekend, sitting in her Pyramid and taking care of the Amazons. And Bushy invited us for a cruise on Sunday afternoon — not a party, just a quiet time on the water. I thought that was very sweet of him, and Thelma said it was just what she needed. We came home and she retired early, and the rest is kind of a blur."

"You've handled everything very well, Janice."

"Yes, but after the doctor had been at the house, I looked in Thelma's handbag, although I felt I was doing something wrong. She was a very private person, you know . . . It was full of money! Bundles of currency! And the little handgun that Mr Simmons insisted on giving her for our cross-country trip. She wanted to give it back to him when he was here, but he wouldn't take it . . . So then I went looking for the pocket tape-recorder he brought her as a gift. It was in the top drawer of her dresser."

"Had she used it?"

"Yes," Janice said with a frightened stare.

"Did you listen to what was recorded?"

"Yes. And that's why I'm here — to ask you what to do with these things of Thelma's."

"Before I can advise you," Qwilleran said solemnly, "I'd better hear the tape."

"Why, Auntie! What are you doing here at this hour? You should be home, getting your beauty sleep — not that you need it! You're beautiful — for your age!"

"Wipe that oily smile off your face, Dickie Bird, and explain who gave you permission to turn Thelma's Film Club into a gambling casino and porno gallery. Next, you'll be renting rooms by the hour!"

"Why, Auntie —!"

"Where's the silver tray you used to have here?"

"I never had a silver tray."

"You're a liar as well as a thief! How much of that money you're counting goes in the club account and how much into your pocket? You're fired! As of now! I want you off the premises in half an hour. And my guest room is no longer at your disposal! You'll find your belongings in a box on the back porch."

"You've got me all wrong!"

"Then tell me what you did with a hundred thousand dollars' worth of jewels that you took from your kidnapping accomplice after killing him on a country road in Bixby. And tell me what happened to your muddy hiking boots that you wore when you pushed your father over the cliff? Your own father who loved you so much and gave you everything you wanted! You had the unmitigated callousness to go home and notify the police that he hadn't come home to lunch! He was my brother! And I'm the only one who cares! . . . You . . . are a monster!"

"You're cracking up, Auntie!"

"Then you came out to Hollywood and put on your loving-nephew act until I changed my will and made you my sole heir . . . Well, I'm going to change it again! And you're not getting a penny!"

"You selfish old woman! You're not going to live long enough to change your will —"

"And you're not going to live long enough to inherit!"

(Two gunshots.)

(Click.)

When the tape ended, Qwilleran said firmly, "Show everything to Mavis Adams as soon as possible. She knows the law, and Thelma was her client."

"Did I do right, Qwill?"

"Yes, but you don't need to tell anyone that you brought it over here. Show everything to Mavis . . . and don't worry. May I freshen your drink?"

"No, thanks. This is a big load off my mind. Now I want to go home and . . . maybe try sitting in Thelma's Pyramid."

"One question, Janice. Did Thelma have a chance to sign her new will?"

"Yes. She'd been working on it with Mavis, and was due to sign it Saturday morning. Mavis brought it to the house. Thelma left everything to a foundation that will reestablish the Thackeray Clinic as a memorial to her dear Bud."

There were two thumps in the kitchen, as Koko jumped down from the top of the refrigerator.

Qwilleran thought, He's been listening to this whole scenario! . . . Did he recognize Dick's voice on the tape? NO! He's never met Smiley; he's just sensed his evil presence.

Koko stared pointedly at his empty plate under the kitchen table, and Qwilleran gave him a little something.

Qwilleran himself had a dish of ice cream. Then he sprawled in his big chair to think. He could imagine Simmons's reaction to the drama. The tape recorder had been an inspired idea.

When Thelma confronted her nephew and he said she wouldn't live long enough to change her will, she knew there was a gun in the desk drawer and she had told Simmons about it.

Did Thelma know all along that Dick was no good? It was too bad that Simmons had to leave so soon. Qwilleran would have enjoyed telling him of Koko's investigative exploits.

It was a curious fact that lawmen were the only ones who accepted Koko's peculiar talents. There had been Lieutenant Hames, Down Below, and there was Brodie, the Pickax police chief. Qwilleran had a hunch that Simmons would have been a third. Too late now.

Koko knew the man was thinking about him. The cat was sitting on a nearby lamp table, squeezing his eyes. He also rubbed his chin on the bottom edge of the lampshade. It was a gesture that seemed to give him a catly thrill. Knocking books off a shelf was another of Koko's quirks, although it sometimes appeared as if there might be a method in his madness.

In the last two or three weeks he had shown a fondness for books with "Richard" in the title. And he had exhibited a sudden interest in Robert Louis Stevenson. In quick succession he had dislodged *Treasure Island* and *Travels with a Donkey* and *Dr Jekyll and Mr Hyde*. Now, Qwilleran felt a prickling sensation on his upper lip. He thought, Could it be that Koko was looking for *Kidnapped*? It was the only Stevenson favorite not on the shelf. The notion, of course, was preposterous. And yet . . .

Qwilleran thought, if the kidnapping connection is preposterous, how about the catfit he staged when we played *The Gambler*? We thought it was Prokofiev's music he didn't like. More likely he was trying to tell us something about Thelma's nephew . . . Koko knows a skunk when he smells one!

"Yoww-ow-ow!" Koko declaimed impatiently and rubbed the lampshade once more.

It was then that Qwilleran noticed an envelope on the table addressed simply to "Qwill." It was large and square and ivory colored, and Qwilleran was not surprised to find the initials "T.T." embossed on the flap. Obviously, Janice had left it there.

Inside there was a sheet of blank white paper.

Dubiously and reluctantly and even furtively, Qwilleran removed the lampshade and passed the paper back and forth over the hot lamp bulbs.

Gradually the message materialized printed in large block letters: THANKS, DUCKY, FOR EVERYTHING.

And where had Koko gone? He was under the kitchen table staring at his empty plate — the one on the right.

Yum Yum sat huddled on her brisket, guarding her one-and-only treasure, her silver thimble.

ISIS publish a wide range of books in large print, from fiction to biography. Any suggestions for books you would like to see in large print or audio are always welcome. Please send to the Editorial department at:

ISIS Publishing Ltd.
7 Centremead
Osney Mead
Oxford OX2 0ES
(01865) 250 333

A full list of titles is available free of charge from:
Ulverscroft large print books

(UK)	**(Australia)**
The Green	P.O Box 953
Bradgate Road, Anstey	Crows Nest
Leicester LE7 7FU	NSW 1585
Tel: (0116) 236 4325	Tel: (02) 9436 2622

(USA)	**(Canada)**
1881 Ridge Road	P.O Box 80038
P.O Box 1230, West Seneca,	Burlington
N.Y. 14224-1230	Ontario L7L 6B1
Tel: (716) 674 4270	Tel: (905) 637 8734

(New Zealand)
P.O Box 456
Feilding
Tel: (06) 323 6828

Details of **ISIS** complete and unabridged audio books are also available from these offices. Alternatively, contact your local library for details of their collection of **ISIS** large print and unabridged audio books.